Author of Eastern hunters

The Gage of Honour - A Tale of the Great Mutiny

Vol. III

Author of Eastern hunters

The Gage of Honour - A Tale of the Great Mutiny
Vol. III

ISBN/EAN: 9783337023270

Printed in Europe, USA, Canada, Australia, Japan

Cover: Foto ©Andreas Hilbeck / pixelio.de

More available books at **www.hansebooks.com**

THE GAGE OF HONOUR.

VOL. III.

THE GAGE OF HONOUR.

A Tale of the Great Mutiny.

BY

THE AUTHOR OF 'THE EASTERN HUNTERS,' &c.

IN THREE VOLUMES.

VOL. III.

LONDON:

TINSLEY BROTHERS, 18, CATHERINE ST., STRAND.

1869.

THE GAGE OF HONOUR.

CHAPTER I.

'Let him but live, and both are Thine,
Together Thine—for blest or crost,
Living or dead, his doom is mine,
And, if *he* perish, both are lost!'—*Lalla Rookh.*

I DO not propose entering into any of those revolting details which characterized so many outbreaks. If the imagination of any of my readers is so morbid as to require such stimulating food, I refer them to the Indian newspapers of the time. In some of those painful narratives the most exacting seeker of the unwholesome excitement of pure sensationalism will find enough to gratify a jaded appetite. At the same time, to that gratification will be added the knowledge that fact there stands for fiction.

All who escaped from the first attack made off towards the fort. Some skirted the cantonments, some dashed right through, and others again sought, by a circuitous route in the country, or across the river, to gain the object of their flight.

The General with all of his staff reached it in safety, as did most of those with whom my narrative has specially dealt. But poor Captain Goodall never made his appearance. He was shot down before he cleared the parade-ground;

Douglas at the same time narrowly escaping by the speed of his horse. But he had the satisfaction of pistolling the man who, as far as he could judge in the confused *mêlée*, was Goodall's actual murderer.

The course of my tale, however, leads me to another quarter.

According to a custom recently established, St Clair had, a short time before the events just narrated, ridden forth with a small party of a dozen Sikh troopers to patrol the various roads between the fort and cantonments. On this occasion he first took that which led most directly from the town towards the isolated dwellings of the two principal civil officers, intending thereafter to sweep round and inspect the others.

It was the last evening on which Mr Selby was to remain in his house; but he was anxious to stick to his post as long as was possible, and his daughter had absolutely refused to leave him. Mrs Atherton had a day or two previously taken possession of tents pitched for her under the fort walls, and had unavailingly endeavoured to persuade her friend Norah to accompany her. Miss Selby would on no account desert her father, and the latter was fully persuaded that the mutiny was not so imminent as it proved to be.

As Major St Clair rode meditatively on, followed by his handful of troopers, his attention was aroused by what seemed the suppressed and distant hum of men in front. This was almost immediately followed by a streak of vivid light which shot up into the air from the direction of cantonments. Hastily calling on his men, he trotted forward, and soon the signal-gun roared forth its summons to plunder and murder, and additional flames announced the further progress of destruction.

The human hum in front now changed into the noisy turmoil of a shouting multitude, and St Clair knew that Mr Selby's house was attacked. As he now rapidly approached, the glare of torches, and shortly flames from the burning outhouses, lighted the way. The dwelling itself, being an old palace of two storys, flat roofed, and firmly cemented, without any thatch, was not so easily ignitible as more ordinary bungalows.

St Clair was aware that a small guard of seven men was located on the basement of the building, and he remembered with satisfaction that these were of his own regiment, under an old duffedar he had specially selected. Inimical as the Sikh is, equally to Mussulman as Hindoo, they had little chance of quarter in case of capture, and would fight to the last. But what were so few against the host now shouting and firing in front of the house, intent, apparently, on assaulting the front door?

Every now and then, indeed, a yell announced that a shot fired from some of the windows had told. This was answered by a volley from the insurgents, which rattled harmlessly against the massive walls of the house. One or two casualties thus incurred among the ranks of the assailants had, however, taught them caution, and they were debating, at a respectable distance from the said door, the propriety of a general and simultaneous rush upon it.

It was at this juncture that St Clair wheeled his little band round a bend in the avenue, and had the scene before him. It was at once apparent to him that the cohesive power and combination of disciplined troops was quite wanting, and that the assailants were composed entirely of city rabble. Many of them were, however, armed with matchlocks and muskets, and kept up a constant fusilade, wild and apparently purposeless, save to animate themselves and others by the sound of their own fire-arms.

All within the house was dark, and gave no indications of the positions of the defenders, but for the occasional shots I have mentioned. St Clair thought that if he could surprise the assailants, by taking them in rear unperceived till close upon them, he would be able to create a temporary panic, and, while that lasted, effect a lodgment in the house. He never seemed to dream of any other course than at once relieving the small and harassed garrison. He pictured to himself the inmates and their distress, and sought only for the best means to join them.

Once there, he could act as circumstances dictated. At present the absolute necessity of his junction with the defenders seemed a matter about which there could be no room for doubt or hesitation.

But he feared to advance within the disc of light from the burning out-houses. His approach would be surely discovered too soon to enable him to act as he desired. He accordingly gave orders to dismount and tether the horses in an orange-grove by the side of the road. This done, he briefly explained to the men his intentions, and told them to fire their carbines upon the insurgents when he gave the word, and then rush in with drawn swords, and fight their way to the grand door. He relied on the suddenness and boldness of the onslaught to clear the way. The unknown number of the assailants, and nature of the attack, would he reckoned frighten the rabble crew, who would probably in their confusion leave them free ingress to the house.

Creeping cautiously forward through the groves and among the trees, he led his men unperceived till they reached a strip of shrubbery which bounded the open green in front of the house.

The insurgents were evidently about to make a fresh assault on the door, and St Clair saw that no time was to be lost. Drawing his men up in line, in extended order, so as to present as imposing a front as possible, he led them to the full extent of the shadow thrown by the neighbouring trees, and then directed them to take careful aim, and fire into the mass of men before them.

They did so ; and on St Clair shouting out, ' Charge ! ' they rushed forward, yelling like madmen, and cutting and slashing, as a true Sikh rejoices to do. The effect was almost instantaneous. Completely taken by surprise, and seeing several of their number drop to the first fire, the rest of the rebels, panic-stricken, broke and fled in every direction.

Some who were not quick enough fell under the keen blades of the Sikhs, and hardly one raised hand in opposition. Without the loss of a man, St Clair and his party reached the door. St Clair soon made his object known to the garrison, if, indeed, the sudden dispersion of the assailants had not prepared them for relief. Before, however, admittance could be given, the startled rebels had somewhat recovered their panic at seeing the small number of their adversaries, and a dropping fire from various directions was opened on them. But before they sufficiently rallied for any combined purpose, the new-comers were admitted, and the massive door was again made fast.

The grim, bronzed old soldiers, under their duffedar, gravely welcomed their loved commandant, and to his inquiries made brief report. 'No casualties as yet. Selby Sahib and the brave Missy baba safe in another room.' And St Clair observed that the young lady's name was referred to in terms of admiration and reverence. The bearded old warriors stood in respectful silence as they listened to St Clair's directions. Their faith in him was unbounded. The former garrison now felt relieved entirely of all further responsibility. The father of the regiment, the great and honoured Major Sahib, had arrived, and everything must of necessity go right, somehow or other. All they had to do was to obey his orders in the strictest manner. For the rest, he would arrange, and make all come right in the end.

Sending the men to their posts, St Clair now sought Mr Selby, to acquire all the information he could, and ascertain if he had formed any plans of his own.

He found father and daughter sitting with hands clasped one within that of the other, in a sheltered situation, on the watch near the window of the room. A couple of fowling-pieces lay ready loaded beside them. From one of these the high-spirited girl had herself fired when the first attack was made on the door, and the danger seemed imminent. One or two trusty servants remained with them, but others had escaped to the insurgents.

A trooper had been detailed to the charge of the window along with them. But on observing the approach of the relieving party, Mr Selby had sent him to the door, while he and his daughter remained on guard.

St Clair was received with expressions

of deep gratitude, and he felt well repaid by the warm and thankful pressure of the girl's hands as she took his offered one in both of hers.

Brief and hasty question and answer elicited the information that the rebels had secretly mustered in force before any within were aware of their approach. Mr Selby had at first intended sending his daughter with one of the Sikhs, as rower and escort, in a small skiff which at most held two, and was secreted under some bushes on the river bank. Dangerous though such a measure was, he hoped by these means to get his daughter safely conveyed to the fort, and at the same time warn them there of his situation. But unfortunately the old troopers had been more accustomed to handle weapons of war than more peaceful oars or paddles, and knew nothing of boats or their management. Mr Selby himself was no oarsman, and, moreover, lacked the strength to undertake the duty. He felt, too, unwilling to leave his brave defenders. He now proposed that St Clair should take on himself to do this, and—if successful in placing his daughter in safety—return with what force he could muster, and escort the besieged to the fort.

St Clair was at first most averse to the plan. He could not, he said, leave his men. But brief reflection served to assure him that, after all, it was the only arrangement which promised success, especially as regarded the gentle Norah. He was a man actuated by a strong sense of duty, but it would be incorrect to assert that his deep desire to be the means of protecting and saving the poor child did not exert a paramount influence.

He dreaded with a bitter, loathing dread, the very idea of her falling into the hands of the insurgents. Should the Sepoys come to the aid of the rabble now outside; or should the latter bring up a field-piece or two from cantonments, the house would be rendered untenable. In that case, the men might take to the river, and make what efforts at escape they could. But the girl would be help-less. In the event of neither Sepoys nor guns being brought to assist in the attack, he felt pretty confident that his well-tried troopers, now eighteen in number, would be able to keep the assailants at bay till he could bring up the rest of his regiment to their relief. Another circumstance also occurred to him. His place of duty was in command of his regiment, which could be rendered much more serviceable under his personal authority at a time when, in all probability, there was great confusion both within and without the fort walls. The men themselves, too, might be disinclined to act without the orders of their immediate superior.

At last, therefore, he signified his readiness to do as required. But now an objection rose from a fresh quarter.

Mr Selby and St Clair had hurriedly arranged the matter between themselves, and at once communicated the proposed . plan to the person most interested.

'I cannot go,' said Miss Selby, when her father announced this decision. 'Oh, darling, do not drive me from you! I will die with you if necessary. Let me remain. Assistance will surely come. God will help us.'

The poor girl not only instinctively felt a maidenly scruple—still with woman's perverseness, influential in that hour of danger—at being convoyed by St Clair, but also shrunk from the idea of leaving her loving old father to his own fate.

'Norah,' said her father, 'I thought you were a courageous and sensible girl. This

good and brave man has agreed with me
that our plan is wisest. He is the best
. able to take care of you and bring his men
to my assistance. We are losing precious
time. I command you, as your father, to
do as I bid you.'

The gentle little old man, usually so·
quiet and obedient to every whim of his
child, was now the firm and determined
father, insisting on his right of exacting
obedience to his own expressed wishes.

She could no more refuse. Clinging
in his embrace, she only uttered a few
passionate words of love and affection,
and then whispered something in his ear.
During this brief colloquy St Clair had
stood, with looks averted from the two,
silent and motionless. But he was cog-

nizant of the start Mr Selby gave at his daughter's whispered words.

'I have thought of it, love,' he heard him reply, 'but I hardly expected you to propose it. It shall be as you wish.'

Turning to St Clair, Mr Selby took him aside, and whispered in his turn in his companion's ear,

'Whatever comes, she must not fall into the rebels' hands. In the very last— *the very last*—when all hope of saving her is gone, then, as her father, I sanction—I take on myself the whole burden—of— her—death.'

The old man's voice trembled as he spoke, and the tears fell from his eyes, but the listener could not doubt that what he said was meant.

St Clair bowed his head in acquiescence, for he, too, had forced himself to a consideration of the terrible alternative. He said simply,

'I understand you to mean that sooner than allow her to fall into the rebels' hands I must destroy her.'

And he placed his hand on the butt of his revolver.

'Does she acquiesce?'

'She does,' was the reply, 'and demands it imperatively as the price of her leaving me.'

'So be it,' gravely returned St Clair. He could speak no more.

There was no time for more to be said on the subject. And St Clair calling to the duffedar, and going round to his men,.

briefly explained his intentions. He urged on them to keep a wary look-out; and, in event of no longer being able to hold the house, get over the river with Mr Selby as best they could, and take to the open country. He then directed them to open a brisk fire so as to cover his present movements.

In the mean time Miss Selby had thrown over her shoulders a dark shawl, so as to conceal the light colour of her dress, and stood prepared for her perilous voyage. Descending the steps which led to the river from a postern in the rear of the house, St Clair drew from its place of concealment the little skiff, and, placing his companion in the stern, took the oars and stepped in. Pushing out a little into the stream, he, with two or three vigorous strokes, soon cleared the length of the house. But away from its shadow the glare of the burning outhouses fell on the water, and there he was afraid to use his oars for fear of attracting attention from any stray men on the bank. Partly screened by the latter, he let the boat drop noiselessly down with the current, only venturing to use his oars to guide its way, and prevent it from becoming entangled with the bushes which drooped into the water.

Leaning forward, he whispered to his companion, 'Whatever happens, you must do as I tell you directly and exactly. Will you promise to obey?'

'Yes!' was the reply.

'Keep perfectly quiet and sit as low in the boat as possible. The principal danger will be within the next few hundred yards after we get to the bend of the river. Keep a good look-out on the bank, and tell me of everything you see move.'

The actual moment of leaving had been so far favourable that the attention of the assailants was just then specially devoted to the front of the house. They were reassembling in the groves on the city road, evidently hesitating to approach near the garrison, whose additional strength was to be discerned in the number of shots which, according to St Clair's directions, were fired on his departure. Any stray man, however, coming down to get water might observe them.

In that case it was St Clair's intention to pull to the opposite side, and seek the open country.

Keeping bent as low in the boat as he possibly could, leaving him, at the same time, power to guide it, he let it drift down the stream. Once or twice they touched some shallow or projecting piece of land or bush; but, fortunately, the deep channel kept for some distance under the left bank, by which they were gliding, and the latter thus partially screened them from observation.

With feelings of grave satisfaction St Clair found that the boat was drifting out of the brilliant irradiation cast by the burning stables, and that ere long he should be able to take to his oars and pull. There was in most parts sufficient water for a small boat to proceed uninterruptedly; but in the channel the current was strongest, and at the next bend it crossed to the other side. Once there, he could make good way, and after the light was passed, with less risk of exposure.

They were now approaching the banyan-tree near the ferry of which I have before spoken, and St Clair thought he might take the oars and pull, when Miss Selby leaned forward, and touching him with her hand, said in a whisper, 'I see some men on the bank lower down. I think there are some in the water.'

St Clair at once checked the boat and drew it in to the bank. The few men in front discerned by Norah were soon joined by others, and the hum of voices announced that a considerable party was assembling. He judged at once that it was at the ferry, and immediately divined that their object was to take up the ferry-boat, probably to assist in the attack on the bungalow from the water.

They had attained a dangerous proximity, and as St Clair cautiously moved the boat in closer and endeavoured to conceal it by the overhanging boughs of the bushes, his heart beat almost audibly. Every second he half expected to hear the exulting shout which should announce their discovery. For one brief moment he thought of pulling across at once, and run the risk of being seen, and chased on the other side. Had he been alone he might possibly have done so. But second thoughts induced him to remain where he was.

All doubt as to the purpose of the insurgents was soon removed. The ferry-boat was secured, and a number of men prepared to drag it up-stream by wading in the shallow water on the other side, where the current was lighter.

Whispering to her what appeared to be the intention of their enemies, St Clair told his companion to sit down in the bottom of the boat, he himself stretching himself there also. His easy uniform was of that light colour and material which is called 'khakee,' and to conceal this he drew a portion of her dark-coloured shawl over his own shoulders. Thus united, she resting in innocent reliance against his strong frame, they awaited the next move in the great game of life against death.

'If they discover us,' he said softly in her ear, 'I shall try and get with you to the other side if I can. But if all escape is cut off, do you really wish for death rather than fall into their hands? Think for a moment before you decide. Are you prepared?'

'There can be but one choice,' she answered firmly. 'Death is infinitely preferable. I am prepared for the worst.'

'You—you forgive me for what I must do?' and as St Clair spoke his frame shook with the agony of his spirit.

'Forgive!' she whispered in a voice so pitying and loving as to express how needless was such a demand. 'But, oh! cannot you save yourself?'

'I would rather die with you than live to see you in their hands,' he said. ' I love you more than all the world.'

'Kiss me,' she said. 'It may be the last pledge of earthly love. But our spirits will meet.'

Her head fell on his breast, and their hands instinctively clasped each other as he wound his arm round her, and bent his face to kiss her.

The world, and all its hopes, and fears, and joys, and sorrows might be passing away, but in that dread hour of peril each felt, as their lips met, that spirit had touched spirit. The imminence of a deadly danger had not, in that moment, the power to overcome that ecstasy of the soul, the greatest of which, humanly speaking, it is susceptible. Standing as the pair were, on the very threshold of another life, when the dread summons to appear before the throne of Him who made them, might even now be on the point of issue, their love was invested with a ‘holiness and purity, partaking more of heaven than earth. Soul cleaved to soul, in the strong cohesion of natural affinity.

‘Pray,’ she gently whispered, and he responded by pressing her more closely to him.

No further word was spoken. Both

were calm, and he resolute. Whether or not the act he meditated were morally wrong, he could not then mentally argue. He felt that her death were more to be desired than her capture. In the latter case her fate was too horrible to dwell upon. That must be averted. And he prayed earnestly for forgiveness if erring human judgment dared, in dire extremity, to arrogate to itself the functions of shaping the end.

The contemplation of the deed itself was agonizing. But it must be.

And Norah! She felt how dreadful for him must be that contemplation, and she momentarily dwelt, in her unselfishness, on relieving him from that terrible duty. But she knew it would be useless

to urge it. As for the rest, doubly dear
though life would now be to her, it were
not so very fearful to pass to another
world, her spirit accompanied by his.

In the mean time the purpose of the
insurgents became fully developed. The
large ferry-boat had been unmoored, and
by dint of hard pushing and pulling by
those wading, the whole accompanied by
much noise, they managed to drag it
slowly on in the shallow water on the
other side.

Nearer and nearer it came, and one of
the watchers in deep suspense marked its
onward progress. The face of the other
was buried in his breast, and its light
form supported by his arm.

The width of the water-channel, then

flowing, was, at the point they occupied, not more than fifty or sixty yards, and he keenly watched for the first indication of their discovery as the rebel band arrived nearly opposite.

Suddenly there arose a shout, and the girl clung with a nervous dread more closely to him.

'Don't fear,' he whispered. 'It is nothing.'

In fact, the only torch carried by one of the waders had fallen into the water and become extinguished, and St Clair's hopes rose with its fall. There was indeed light enough thrown on the opposite side for the men there employed to do their work uninterruptedly. But the bank under which the little skiff lay concealed was more in shadow, and the extinction of the torch diminished their chances of detection.

The working party brought the boat opposite, and then they passed, and still no signs of discovery. Each minute increased the distance, and at last St Clair whispered in the ear of the trembling child he held in his arms that 'the danger was past.'

As he spoke her slender form seemed inclined to slip from him, and he anxiously asked if she were faint.

'Only a little,' she replied in a low voice, endeavouring at the same time to rouse herself.

He dipped his hand in the water, and sprinkled it over her face. On her as-

suring him that she was revived, he again
kissed her, and telling her to take her old
seat, made his own preparations to con-
tinue the voyage.

He pushed the boat once more into
the stream, and still hugging the bank,
let it drop down. On approaching the
ford, he pulled out into the middle, and
with vigorous strokes sent the light boat
flying through the water.

The channel shortly crossed to the
other side, and with a deep sigh of relief
he told her the greatest danger was over,
for there would be little likelihood of
meeting enemies in the gardens on the
banks, so far from the present attraction
afforded by the looting of the bungalows.

Setting steadily to work, St Clair now

made rapid progress, and soon the fort,. with many lights glancing in and about it, came fully into view. Another few minutes brought them opposite the line of entrenchment containing the camp of his own regiment, between which and the fort, immediately under the walls, were pitched numerous tents for the use of the fugitives from cantonments.

'Who cum dar?' was shouted in loud tones as the boat-splash attracted the attention of a sentry, and a rattle of small arms showed that the river was well watched.

'English fugitives,' returned St Clair in Hindustanee. 'Major St Clair and a lady.'

A howl went up into the night on

this announcement.   It was answered by
shouting as the news of the arrival spread,
and by mingled cries of—

'The great Major is safe!'   'Praise
to the Holy One and the good Gooroo!
the father has returned to his children.'

Pulling in to the landing-place, St
Clair was warmly welcomed by his own
troopers and many of the fugitive officers,
who were taking their tour of duty as
ordinary sentries.

Directing his men to mount and fall
in, stating that he had some work for
them, St Clair turned to assist his companion to land.

She was faint and weak from the
dreadful ordeal she had undergone; but
the deep anxiety she still felt for her

father, and her own natural spirit and pluck—it is the most expressive word—sustained her.

The fierce warlike natures of the Sikh soldiers softened, and they made way respectfully as St Clair assisted the fragile girl towards the tent of Mrs Atherton, which he inquired for and soon found. Leaving her to the tender care of her loving friend, with brief words of comfort and assurances of shortly bringing her father to her, he sought the General—who had reached the fort,—and received permission to take a squadron of his men to the assistance of Mr Selby and his brave defenders. But he was at the same time directed not to run any risk of much loss by engaging any large body of Sepoys.

Every fighting man was precious in their scant garrison.

Naturally there was no little confusion about the fort; but St Clair found his men ready drawn up. He enforced strict attention to his orders, and loved as he was by the men, his influence was manifested in their high state of discipline. Several of the officers also volunteered to accompany him, and he accepted the offers of some half-dozen.

Most of them longed to wreak even such retaliation as a few pistol-shots or sword-cuts might give them the means of doing. Revenge and race hatred were not unnaturally aroused by the events of the night.

St Clair was soon mounted, and led

his men at a brisk trot down the road towards the Residency. The whole cantonment was now in flames, which cast a lurid glare on the trees of the avenue as they trotted down it. But no roar of artillery sounded, and St Clair felt persuaded that Mr Selby's garrison still held out, for he could distinguish a dropping fire in its direction.

Many of the men who followed him were bronzed and rugged veterans who had manfully opposed us at Ferozeshah and Sobraon, and, later still, at Chillianwallah and Gujerat. They had proved themselves the bravest and most warlike race of India, and from having once been sturdy enemies, had now become, in the time of our great need, trusty friends.

Little thought they of the despised Pandies, and as for sabreing a lot of city rabble, however numerous, it was mere child's play.

They had a lingering hope, too, that those they were about to attack might, possibly, be not unprovided with something worth capturing. 'Loot' is a household word, and one full of charm to your true Sikh. The very indefiniteness of what may be acquired has all the attraction of a gambling transaction, with everything to gain and nothing to stake—unless the trifling risk of one's life be so regarded by the less warlike.

Thus impressed, the men rode merrily on, eager for a brush, and confident in their leader.

The vicinity of the Residency was soon reached. The horses of the patrol were first found as left, and untethered, and then St Clair, deploying into as broad a front as the space permitted, led off at a sharp pace. In another minute they galloped in amongst the insurgent horde with a battle-shout which would not have disgraced the British throat.

Down went men, and arms and turbans rolled in the dust as the horsemen pressed spurring in among the throng of footmen hampered by their very numbers. Their blows fell thick and fast, for the sword only was employed. Many of the rebels unhurt, too, were cast down and trampled under-foot. All who could fly, fled; and ere long the insurgent band, including many Sepoys, had dissolved like a snow-wreath in summer.

Some sought the groves and fields. Others swam the river or made for the ferry-boat, which, filled with men, was moored under the terrace-wall. The dispersion was complete, and all opposition over in a few minutes. As soon as the relieved garrison came out and joined their comrades, they first inquired after the safety of the 'great Major Sahib' and the brave young Missee. That done, grim jokes and hoarse laughs passed on the subject of the imprisonment of the garrison, the ease with which they had been rescued, and the slaughter of the contemptible besiegers. A couple of their own number killed, and half-a-dozen

wounded, was well balanced by some
thirty or forty of the enemy left lying on
the ground.

Mr Selby pressed St Clair's hand with
feelings of the deepest gratitude as he
learnt of his daughter's safety.

Re-assembling his men, who were engaged in rifling the killed and snapping up
such 'unconsidered trifles' as took their
fancy, St Clair divided his little force
into two parties. One of these he despatched direct to the fort in charge of
Mr Selby and the wounded men; and
determined with the other to patrol towards the cantonments, and endeavour
to aid whoever might yet be lingering on
the road, or have sought concealment
near it.

CHAPTER II.

' Yes, love, indeed, is light from heaven ;
    A spark of that immortal fire
    With angels shared, by Alla given
    To lift from earth our low desire.'—*The Giaour*.

WEARILY and anxiously wore away the hours of the night. Many were missing; and though some of these were known to have been killed, the fate of others was uncertain. Unable to make their way direct, they might be wandering about in the country or hiding.

The little garrison remained under arms all night, vigilant and prepared.

Fatigue parties worked at the entrenchments which defended the camp, so as to
render them deeper and more difficult to
be assailed. A small, rough earthwork,
too, was thrown up, and a couple of
howitzers placed in position, so as to
sweep the approaches. In fact, every pre-
caution was taken to render the position
as strong and tenable as circumstances
permitted. It was not expected that the
Sepoys, who had only a couple of batteries of field-pieces, would make any prolonged attack on the fort, with the object
of its capture by siege ; but they might
possibly make a demonstration, and, unless warmly received, endeavour to carry
it or the entrenchments by a *coup-de-main*.
After St Clair's return a chain of vedettes

was established, so as to give immediate intimation of the approach of any enemy. These, with constant patrols and fatigue work, kept the Sikhs pretty fully employed.

Day dawned at length; and with the advent of light many sought that rest which the uncertainty and vagueness attaching to darkness rendered impossible.

All minor efforts now culminated in the formation of a patrol—including a number of officers in its ranks—of sufficient force to scour the country round about, undeterred by the opposition of any small band of rebels. Should the latter appear in force, or should any symptoms of approach towards the fort be discerned, St Clair was directed to return at once, and under no circumstances to go so far as to render his doing so very hazardous.

This was effected with some moral effect on the neighbouring villages, and the succour of several fugitives, both English and native; many of them wounded.

In one or two of the nearest villages— the only ones his instructions allowed him to visit—he found that carriage was being collected for the rebels, and consequently that their early departure might be looked for. But on his return he observed movements near the cantonments, which he thought indicated a disposition to make a demonstration in force in the direction of the fort.

A small party of the rebel cavalry hastily fled as he approached, but without making any effort at pursuit, he returned to report his suspicions.

These were verified soon after midday, when the insurgent force was seen from the fort walls advancing in columns by the various roads, and in fair array and order. They were suffered to approach till they debouched on to an open space, and prepared to deploy. On one or two of these spots the fort guns had been previously accurately trained, and the order was now given to open fire.

This was done, and with such effect that the rebels withdrew after firing a few ineffectual shots from their field-pieces.

It was probably merely a demonstration, made to satisfy the vanity of the leaders, and, in a manner, as an assertion of their superiority, and power to act as they chose. At any rate, on the following morning the cantonment was found to be evacuated, and it was soon ascertained that the mutineers had marched, a couple of hours before dawn, on the road which led to Sungumpore, the capital of the neighbouring native principality.

Re-possession was at once taken, a strong picket posted there, and the cantonment cleared of marauding townspeople and villagers, with but small regard for their persons.

These had collected, like jackals, to the remnants of the lion's feast, when the Sepoy providers had left. They were

found in the act of completing the demo-
lition of what remained, and rummaging
among the *débris* for whatever of portable
property they might discover.

But the pretty cantonment itself, how
changed! Most of the bungalows, being
thatched, had proved easy prey to the in-
cendiaries; and what remained of them
now stood disfigured and blackened
masses of sun-dried brick. Gables rose,
grim and naked, among crumbling ruins,
in all their desolate ugliness; and charred
beams here and there protruded their
burnt ends. The ashes on the trampled
gardens and the smoke-blackened trees—
in some instances themselves partially con-
sumed—indicated where gigantic bon-
fires of furniture and other ignitable

things, too bulky for removal, had been made. Stray household articles, whole or in pieces, with broken carriages, were scattered far and wide. With these were mingled clothes, bottles, crockery, jars, and all the various necessaries of domestic luxury and comfort which an English residence in India contains. Amidst the *débris* roamed dogs and poultry engaged in searching for food. The very jackdaws and minars seemed to feel the scene of desolation as they sat blinkingly regarding it, or hopped about the blackened ruins in wondering curiosity.

The sad and mournful duty of searching for the dead was soon accomplished, and the victims committed to their untimely graves.

Anxious and troubled was the time for all. But the days sped on; weeks passed into months, and things dropped gradually into the easy groove of use and habit. Detachments of troops were pushed on, and arrived in due course; and General Marston only waited for the main body to reach him to organize a field force. With this he proposed to advance on Sungumpore, or meet the enemy, should they come—as it was asserted they would—to attack him.

The mutinous force had reached that place, and been warmly welcomed by the Rajah; the latter was now busily engaged in completing his preparations for bringing into the field a considerable army of his own ill-trained soldiers, native and foreign. These were destined to act in concert with the valuable and well-disciplined brigade of Sepoys which had cast in their fortunes with his, but remained under their own officers.

Had he at once advanced with a few heavy battering-guns before reinforcements reached the General, it might have gone hard with the fort and its garrison. But the native mind is wonderfully impressed by the possession and presence in action of a number of guns, often as useless for all practical purposes as burdensome in their requirements of transport and protection. However, they have the effect of inspiring confidence by their number, and spirit by their noise.

Thus it happened that the Rajah and

his numerous advisers lost much valuable
time in setting up old pieces on carriages,
some as rickety as many of the guns they
supported were honey-combed.   Native
dilatoriness and want of energy also pro-
voked no little delay, and to this was
subsequently added considerable disunion
caused by jealousy and conflict of opinion
between the small chiefs and leaders, and
the native officers of the Sepoys.

All this the General learnt principally
through the native bankers and shroffs,
and their agents, whose network of communication envelops all India.   His own
spies were abroad also.   Old Heerachund
was now in frequent intercourse with the
General and Mr Selby, and was altogether a gentleman of no little import-

ance. The carriages and horses of himself and family were placed at the disposal of those of the ladies who had lost their own, Miss Selby being especially favoured in this particular. Rides and drives were thus soon resumed, for the city budmashes, or roughs, slunk into the shelter of obscurity. When they found that the Government held its ground, and that instead of the Feringhees being driven into the sea, the latter, on the contrary, appeared to be delivering fresh accessions to their number, they began to feel that they had made some serious miscalculation.

Even had there not been a very sufficient amount of hard, active service in prospect, the time was not one for

marrying or giving in marriage. But
love is tied to neither time nor place.
The happy, innocent blush with which
Norah greeted St Clair at their first meeting in private a few days after the events
of the night which I have recorded, was
dwelt on with rapture by the grave,
middle-aged soldier. Even now he
scarcely believed it possible that the
bright child could really love him—the
worn and rugged-fronted, rusty soldier,
the man of camps, tanned and seamed
with nearly twenty years of hard Indian
service. That the fair young girl should
have selected him on whom to lavish the
wealth of her affections seemed incompre-
hensible. He must have been mistaken.

Yet there she stood in all her sweet

young promise, with her hand left in his, and looking at him—coyly, it is true—but still looking at him with an innocent gaze of love, and faith, and trust. Too simple and natural to make any pretence of concealing what she felt, now that she knew it was reciprocated; she stood before him blushing, but with her whole expression and attitude denoting the vivid nature of her feelings.

He took her other hand in his own left, and raising both pressed them against his ample breast, looking down as he did so into the eyes upturned to his. In their pure love-lit depths, even he—little versed though he was in such matters—saw that he was not mistaken.

'Then you do really love me—me—for

myself, and not from any foolish motives of gratitude.'

'Very, very much,' was her reply. 'I have done so for long. Gratitude has nothing to do with it.'

'My own loved little darling;' and the girlish form was pressed to his, and kisses rained on her yielded lips.

'Hullo! Upon my word!' ejaculated Mr Selby from the tent door. 'What's all this about? Oh, you wicked puss.'

'You know you always said he was one of the finest fellows in India,' replied his daughter, without moving, except to hide her face on St Clair's shoulder. 'And, you know, I was bound as your daughter to believe you.'

'Did you ever hear the like of that?' asked Mr Selby, appealing generally to the chairs and tables.

'Now, don't pretend to be cross, dear. It's all your fault, if there is any. And I'm sure you ought to be grateful to me for having made so good a choice.'

'Well, indeed!' the old gentleman exclaimed, with the very faintest effort to disguise his satisfaction. But he was interrupted by St Clair, who, without releasing his fair burden, said, 'The dear child loves me, sir, as I have long loved her. I trust you have no objections.'

'Ah, oh! Can't say I have any, my dear fellow, to you. But to think of this deceitful puss! Why, would you believe it,' he continued, as he went on with running commentaries of his own, — 'she always gave me to understand "that Major St Clair was so very grave,"—I think she said "old" too ;—"that Major St Clair was so very hard upon her for her flirtations,"—serve her right, the co-quette ; "that Major St Clair was so very unlovable " — save the mark ; " that Major St Clair hated her "—oh, did he ? "that Major St Clair didn't understand women "—Begad ! he's like the rest of his sex ; "that Major St Clair couldn't love a woman, she knew, because he was so wrapped up in his profession "—"that Major St Clair—" '

'Hush ! hush ! ' said a little, sobbing voice, interrupting him. ' That was all long ago. I know you like him. You said he was brave and good, that terrible night, and I began to think so, too, ever such a while ago. There, dear, kiss me and say you are very glad,' and the speaker changed her position from her lover's embrace to that of her father.

'My child!' said Mr Selby, humbly obeying. 'My dearest love, my own bright little Norah! I am indeed well pleased that you should love a good, brave, and true-hearted man, even though he be so very much your senior. I say nothing of the great debt we owe him. There, pet, don't sob so.'

'Thank you, sir,' said St Clair briefly, as he turned towards the door of the tent. 'I will leave you for the present.' So saying, he took his departure, leaving father and daughter alone to-gether.

When St Clair communicated the cir-cumstance to his young friend and relative, Ned Percy, that gentleman was good enough to pat the ' old man '—as he addressed him—encouragingly on the back while he expressed his approval, and there and then stated that the affair had the honour of his complete sanction.

And meeting Miss Selby out riding a few days later, he was so kind as to manœuvre, till he drove off ' old Hugh ' and got her to himself. This effected, he condescended to express himself in a similar style of approbation. But he thought it right to mark his sense of her duplicity, and the defeats, on his part, to which it had led, by a few preliminary observations.

'I thought I was up to a thing or two,' he commenced. 'But I must confess I was never prepared for such a complete misdirection. A sign-post topsy-turvy couldn't be worse than you in misleading. I'll never believe in womankind again.'

'I don't believe you ever could,' answered Miss Selby, pouting a little and tossing her head, 'simply because you don't understand them.'

'To think,' continued Mr Percy, 'that I was in a perfect shiver about the plunger. That I have exerted all my noblest abilities "to point the moral and adorn the tale"—as the doctor said the other evening—of that unfortunate man, and all the time you were laughing in your sleeve.'

'What your noblest abilities may be, I confess my helplessness to discover. But I presume they find their expression in what you call "chaff." Now, mustn't we women have some defensive weapons of our own? You see, we haven't got those "noble abilities," and must rely on other means to protect ourselves, when you lords of the creation oppress us with their magnitude.'

'Ah,' said Mr Percy; and then, after a thoughtful pause, continued, 'That's it, is it? It seems to me that the defence is somewhat stronger than the attack. In this case it has been, at any rate. I confess myself to have been

beaten at all points. You simple inno-
cents have, after all, got a womanly something which a fellow can't understand.
But I forgive you. I give both you and
old Hugh my paternal blessing. There,
there, don't thank me. You have it
freely.'

'Much obliged, I'm sure,' was the
reply, not spoken, however, with such
effusion of gratitude as Mr Percy's words
might have led one to expect. 'No doubt
we shall rightly estimate so very valuable
a benediction. But,' and the girl's voice
changed from its tone of banter to one
more earnest, 'I hope, that is to say,
we have been very good friends, Mr
Percy, and I should like us to remain so.
You don't think it is likely to be other-

wise than productive of happiness to him ?'

'I think,' the lad replied, also in an altered tone, 'that he is an extremely lucky fellow, and that *it*,' laying stress on the word, and smiling as he repeated it, 'that *it* is as likely to bring *him* happiness as anything could. You will have a fine, true-hearted fellow for a husband, and I am heartily glad you have felt and returned his affection. Believe me, his is the love of a man whose affections have not been frittered away in all sorts of loves and milk-and-water sentimentalities. Loving,—depend on it,—he loves with his whole heart, something very differently to the butterflies who flutter round an attractive girl like yourself. And you,

I think, in every way worthy of such a love.'

'Thanks, Ned,' said the girl, warmly, for the first time using his Christian name. 'I believe every word you say about him. And I also believe that you are a dear, good, warm-hearted fellow.'

'Dear little Norah!' returned her companion. 'Whatever I am, I have had enough discernment to detect the beauties of the purity and simplicity of character common to you both. It always seems such a wretched thing to me that so many can never get beyond the outside; such a lot seem to judge human beings by all the mere frivolities of society, or the accidental superiority of birth, or position, or the advantages of dress, and nothing

else. Fancy tailoring and millinery possessing such power in the formation of
thinking men and women. They say it
takes nine tailors to make a man. I
wonder how many tailors' bills it takes to
make up a gentleman? But here comes
old Hugh! I mustn't keep him away
any longer. *He* is not a very first-rate
dresser, is he? However, you will im-
prove him in that respect.'

As the young fellow warmly shook
her offered hand, he thought to himself
that 'old Hugh really was a most lucky
old beggar.' And then as he reflected
on what had passed, he further thought,
'Beaten at all points. Why, here have
I been making long speeches and moral-
izing instead of chaffing her, as I in-

tended! But there is no withstanding the natural charm of the little witch. She can just turn any of us round her finger. There's no mistake about it.'

CHAPTER III.

'And there were sudden partings, such as press
The life from out young hearts, and choking sighs
Which ne'er might be repeated ; who could guess
If ever more should meet those mutual eyes,
Since upon night so sweet such awful morn could rise!'
Childe Harold.

MRS ATHERTON had, as we know, taken great interest in her young friend's love affairs, after the natural instinct of women generally. The recital of that trying boat-voyage had excited her liveliest sympathies. She was now perfectly ready to chaperon her, or do any amount of gooseberry work in Norah's behalf.

She had her own causes for sorrow, but none the less did she interest herself in the fortunes and happiness of the bright young creature she tenderly loved.

But a few months had elapsed since Mr Atherton's murder, and she still felt the unavailing regret for her deviation from a wife's duty to the dead, which had at first so strongly overcome her. And, added to this, was now a sense, an instinctive apprehension rather than a perception, of some alteration in the nature of Douglas' affection.

Not a word had he uttered on the subject. Not the slightest reference had been made by either to what might be in the future, or to that visit to him which, she too surely felt, had, in some degree, changed the current of his feelings.

There now existed no reason to prevent, in process of time, her union with the man she loved. Her circumstances, as the widow of the rich Mr Atherton, were widely different from those of the penniless Miss Fortescue.

It would have been sheer hypocrisy on her part to assume that anticipations of future happiness were extinct, because the husband she had never loved had so recently been taken away. She strove, indeed, to dwell on such thoughts as little as might be, but they would present themselves. Something was, of course, due to the world and its requirements. But a sense of public propriety was powerless to subject private feeling.

Moreover, the present was a time when the arbitrary laws of society were considerably relaxed ; for people had enough to think of besides the business of their neighbours. It, therefore, occasioned little surprise or comment when Mrs Atherton and Miss Selby were frequently escorted in their rides and drives by Douglas as well as St Clair.

But the cold weather was again at hand, and the time fast approaching when the earnest business of the campaign must for long put a stop to such friendly personal intercourse. Numerous movable columns were being formed in different parts, in addition to the large *corps d' armées*, for the purpose of expelling the rebels from certain points, punishing them for their misdeeds, and pacifying the country. General Marston was now nearly prepared to take the field, and the safety of those so precious to loving women be once more thrown on the hazard of battle.

'Ah, would he say one loving word to her before he went?' so Mrs Atherton thought. 'Was his old love so dead as to be pitiless? Could nothing ever compensate for that one irretrievable step which had so lowered her in his estimation? Had the subtle essence of his love been utterly destroyed by that one dereliction from the straight path of rectitude to which her unhappy domestic relations had impelled her? Had her momentary departure from that strict purity and innocence upon which his love had been hitherto mainly founded, annihilated its more refined and therefore more volatile portion ? '

His very conduct on the occasion— now so bitterly regretted — had only served to fix more unalterably the affection she had now no object in restraining. He had saved her from herself, and that fact had on one an effect exactly the reverse of that on the other.

'Could not the old love be regained? It could. It must. The unblemished life of the future must atone for the past. Would the boundlessness of her love elicit no responsive sympathy on his part? Would all the countless hours of grief, and remorse, and tears bring no balm to her

weary spirit, and have no influence upon
him ? Would her devotion not regener-
ate that love which she so prized ? Such
a love could not go unrequited. She
would wrest it fróm him.'

Douglas saw but little of this inter-
nal conflict. He felt, indeed, that she
deeply loved him, though he realized not
to the full the passionate fervour of that
love, now that it was released from all
restraining motives.

At the same time he felt that the best
part of his own love was, as it were, in
abeyance. It might only be slumbering,
not dead. But her seeking his house had,
as he judged it, by its apparent infraction
of all laws of feminine delicacy and propriety, greatly shocked the sensitive feel-

ings he entertained on the subject of women. However, he had the best of all remedies for unpleasant thought—good hard work.

The camp containing the field-force destined for active operations was pitched on that plain near cantonments, which was the opening scene of this story. Every preparation had been made for an immediate advance, as the enemy had arrived within a few marches, though the whole of the reinforcements had not reached the General.

A field-mess had been formed for the staff, and one evening Douglas entered this somewhat late, with the information that, in all probability, the camp would break up on the morrow. 'He had,' he said, 'just been closeted with the General regarding the reports which had arrived only a short time before.'

'Hurrah!' exclaimed Percy. 'I, for one, am awfully tired of this inaction. I do so long to have a good go-in at the blackguards. I suppose we shall move now to attack without waiting for the rest of the expected troops.'

'"He jests at scars that never felt a wound,"' observed Dr Cruickshanks. 'Take care, my lad, that the blackguards don't get a good go-in at you. A little blood-letting, though, would not be to your disadvantage.'

'Thanks. Don't quite see it. That's a sort of lowering of the temperature to which, curiously enough, I have a constitutional antipathy.'

'Talking about a good go-in,' said Marryat, the assistant Adjutant-General of the division,—'I strongly suspect the Europeans will give but little quarter if they once get among the mutineers from this. I was looking over the ruins of cantonment the other day, and the vows of revenge scratched on the walls were numerous. "Death to the niggers," and "Remember Cawnpore" were the mildest. Others were couched in vigorous Saxon terms, more expressive than elegant.'

'Yes,' said the chaplain to the force, 'there is no doubt a feeling of deep animosity on the part of the men, and no wonder. But I was much struck with a quotation from the 1st Book of Kings,

written just above the place where the
. *table*
~~altar~~ of the pretty little church stood : *

"They have forsaken thy covenant,
thrown down thine altars, and slain thy
prophets with the sword; and I, even I
only, am left, and they seek my life to
take it away." Not altogether inappro-
priate, I think.'

The nearer the enemy approached the
less difficulty would the General have
in getting at them, and all was held in
readiness for a march to attack them at a
few hours' notice, whenever the time
should arrive. On the evening of the day
subsequent to that just mentioned he
learnt that they had reached the banks of
a river about ten miles from his camp, and

* Fact.

had halted there, perhaps with the intention of waiting for daylight the following morning to enable them to cross over their heavy guns in safety.

He, and many others, knew the spot well, having often shot along the banks of the river, which was celebrated as excellent quail-ground. Native exaggeration had estimated their numbers by tens of thousands. But he calculated that in addition to the brigade of Sepoys, numbering some 3500 men, there might be some three or four thousand Sepoys from other quarters, with perhaps 5000 additional fighting men of various descriptions and merit. To meet these he could place in line nearly 4000 thoroughly reliable troops of all arms, half of whom were

European. Two field batteries—one of horse artillery—and six heavy guns were ready to accompany this column to the field.

This little force, well appointed in every respect, was directed to be ready to march at midnight unembarrassed by anything but the siege-guns and train. Carriage was held in readiness to follow it, in case of the enemy being beaten—a result which, it is needless to say, the General and all under him looked upon as certain. It, however, behoved the former to take such precautionary measures as the possibility of reverse or failure dictated.

But the wary old General knew that to attack, and not wait to be attacked, was

desirable both to animate his own troops,
dishearten the enemy, and inspire the sur-
rounding country with the confidence in
the stability of the British Government
which it was so necessary to create. He
had learnt, too, that now so near, the
Rajah hesitated to advance, and the shrewd
soldier well understood this hesitation.
The white faces had a horrible species of
repulsive fascination for him. He longed
to distinguish himself by their overthrow,
but the very name of white soldier conveyed something of undefined terror to his
mind.

Their bravery, their fierceness in battle,
their terrible ' hoohoohoorar,' when bear-
ing down on the enemy, their relentless
cruelty when in fight, all presented them-

selves in magnified form to his benighted
imagination. Though well acquainted
with English gentlemen, he yet half believed the strange stories which had been
told him of the cannibalism after battle
of the soldiers, and of how dreadfully they
mutilated the slain and tortured the
prisoners. So, when he at last found
himself in close proximity to these terrible devils in battle, his heart somewhat
misgave him, notwithstanding the moral
influence of his numerous guns, and
he determined to accept, rather than
give, battle in his own chosen position.

In anticipation of the night march the
British camp sank early to rest. But
several galloped back to the fort and
entrenchments to bid one last good-bye

before the morrow, and the possible fate
which the God of battles might destine for
them.

St Clair and Douglas rode together,
for their way was the same. The two
ladies were waiting for them, and walked
forth in their company along the river-
bank, each with her separate companion.

Poor Norah remembered now, in the
hour of danger, with much concern, the
reputation her lover had acquired for
dashing bravery. It was this, combined
with his womanly gentleness, and utter
absence of assumption, which had, at first,
so deeply impressed her young imagination. But now the recollection of his
well-proved courage came with feelings,
it is true, of pride, but also of fear. Her

fancy depicted hundreds of imaginary dangers. She imagined him rushing into useless peril and daring all kinds of unnecessary risks.

As she clung in his embrace, she poured forth in his ear her fears and entreaties.

'Why, you foolish baby,' he said cheerfully, 'you seem to think that I am commanding the whole force, and that my principal object is to get myself shot or sabred. I assure you, little one, I have a great objection to either form of death. Why, my own darling! I have no particular desire to rush headlong into every danger which it is possible for the heart of man, or rather of a foolish little woman, to conceive. I shall do my duty. You would not wish me to do less!'

'No, darling. But, then, you may con-
sider all sorts of rash charges and hand-to-
hand fights to be your duty.'

'Don't fear, foolish little bird! I am
neither rash nor foolhardy. Besides, I am
not my own master. I have to obey
orders, and the General is a man who does
not thoughtlessly expose those under him.'

There was some comfort in this, as
Norah reflected that General Marston was
a quiet, mild old gentleman, and that —
what had escaped her—Hugh really was
not the principal individual in the little
army. She was not aware that the General was, though mild, a most determined
old fire-eater where any advantage was
likely to be obtained by enterprise.

Somewhat relieved in mind, therefore, she brought down the head above, by the mere weight of a light arm, and pressing her face to his, said, ' Remember, you have some one else to think of now. Your second self claims her fair share of consideration. For my sake, you must take great care of yourself. I don't think you half know how much I love you.'

' Darling ! my own dearest, best-loved little Norah ! ' These, together with some other foolish expressions, such as simple men will sometimes use on like occasions, were all that was spoken during a considerable pause. The special cause for this interruption having at length come to an end, again she enjoined on him the strictest attention to his own preservation, compatible with what duty demanded. 'I shall be so glad when it is over,' she said. 'I shall pray for my darling. God knows who that is.'

But while the two thus communed, the other pair had strolled away, somewhat further along the river-side. The moon, which was about half full, fell on the stream with its light checkered by the interception of the shadow of several trees which grew on the banks. Myriads of little moonlit wavelets, caused by the current meeting the gentle night-wind, seemed to leap into existence, and dancing their brief span, hurry towards, and then disappear amid, the gloom of the shadows.

Looking on the current thus flowing

past at their feet, neither for a while spoke. At last Mrs Atherton said,

'How happy those two are in their perfect love and faith in one another. Deep, true love must have trust and reliance.'

'Yes,' he replied. 'It must.'

'And it is rich, and forgiving, and has charity,' she said sadly. 'I don't think you can ever have felt it as—as I have.'

'I think I have done so.'

'Ah, "have done." That signifies that it is past and gone. It exists no longer.'

'It exists,' he said gently; 'but in an altered form.'

She glanced up at him quickly with her large gray eyes suffused, then again looked out on the stream as she said, 'Part gone; is the rest worth having?' And then, as he made no reply, continued, 'Are faults committed, sins for ever? Is everything unchangeable? Is an error bitterly, oh how bitterly, repented! irredeemable? Is one false step, committed in the madness of passion and indignation, to stain for ever?'

'No,' he replied. 'But, you know, when an idol is once shattered or defaced, it takes some time to repair.'

'Oh, Frank,' she exclaimed, 'have pity. I once asked you before. I ask again—forgive.' She murmured this in a voice so sad and tender, that his heart was deeply touched. He wondered, too, at the force of that affection which had so metamorphosed the proud, unyielding woman into the humble suppliant. And oh, how very beautiful she looked with the moon burnishing her bright chestnut hair, and lighting her pale face, for she had taken off the hat she had hastily put on before they left the tents.

'Helen! my love!' he .said, as he leant over and kissed her forehead. He had no need to say more. She felt that he was striving to love her with the old love. That though he would not at this time treat her with its outward manifestation, it might come to pass, he would do so in the future. And she felt satisfied and contented. She seized one of his hands, and kissed it repeatedly, as he once more touched her fair, open forehead with his lips, while he muttered as he did so, ' God give you peace.'

It was a little time before he again spoke, which he did on a different subject altogether.

' I wish to place a few things in your hands,' he said, ' in case anything should happen to me to-morrow. Here is a little packet for my sister. And this is one for you. I dare say you will recognize some old friends. There is a dead flower, and a glove in it. A locket also. It was given me by my sister many years ago, and I have put a little piece of my own hair into it in addition to hers. There is a loose lock of hair also. It belonged to a poor unhappy woman who died years ago—one to whom I was of some use.

A very sad story altogether. There are a few other things, and a book or two. Will you wear the locket as the pledge of my affection? You have already what I have always looked upon as the gage of my honour to stand your friend under all circumstances.'

'Ah! How well you have acted up to that gage!' she said. 'Yes. I will wear the locket next my heart till I die; and the other things shall be taken care of till you come back to claim them.'

'Perhaps that will never be,' he said.

'Hush, dear, hush! Don't speak so,' she replied appealingly.

'Do you believe in presentiments?' he asked.

'I—I don't know,' she answered in a scared voice.

He reflected for a few seconds, and then said, 'Yes. It is best you should know it. It will prevent any sudden shock. It is my belief, Helen, that to-morrow will be fatal to me.'

'Oh, don't say that, Frank, dear! For God's sake, banish all such thoughts from your mind. How can any one anticipate what it is reserved for the future to unravel?'

'I have been in action before,' he said, 'under circumstances of greater danger than is likely to attend us to-mor-row; but I have never felt the same depression. You know I come of an old Scotch family, and they have their superstitions. I have seen my wraith—always an omen of ill to us.'

'Frank, Frank, don't speak in that way! It is terrible.'

'My poor Helen! My only reason for telling you is to prepare you for the worst.'

'The worst! Oh, I cannot, dare not think of it! My God, have pity! The punishment would be greater than I could bear.'

'Calm yourself, dear one,' he said soothingly. 'It may but be some wild distemper of the brain. I shall try and shake it off. I thought it, however, right to let you know what my presentiment is. Let us look hopefully forward, trusting in God's mercy. And now I must get back to camp.   Good-bye, Helen, my love!' he murmured, as he once more kissed her forehead, and this time put his arm round and pressed her to him, as he uttered his lingering adieux.

CHAPTER IV.

'K. HEN. O God of battles! steel my soldiers' hearts ;
Possess them not with fear ; take from them now
The sense of reckoning, if the opposing numbers .
Pluck their hearts from them.'—*King Henry the Fifth.*

LONG before midnight the camp was astir. Indeed, portions of it could hardly be said to have been otherwise throughout. The task of loading heavy ammunition—say at a rate of six or eight shot per camel—is one of no mean magnitude, especially on the first occasion, before practice has simplified the operation.

But by twelve the various regiments

and detachments had fallen in, and were being arrayed in their allotted positions on the line of march. The plan and organization had been so well matured, that even on this—the starting march—but little confusion occurred in the dark. Dreadfully wearisome and dreary are those night-marches, when, night after night, the soldier falls in, sleepy and stupid, with no expectation of any excitement to keep up the spirits or enliven the tedious prospect of the next few hours. But with the anticipation of immediate action the case is very different. All are on the *qui vive*. Vigilance assumes the place of intense drowsiness; animated interest that of listless apathy; and cheering expectation the monotony of hopeless prospects.

All looked forward to that day bringing them fairly face to face with the rebels, on terms which, it was expected as hoped, would lead to the exaction of that retribution by the desire of which every Englishman was impressed.

Many a one had to mourn a relative or friend who had fallen either in the mutiny at Hussunabad itself or elsewhere. While among the soldiers, or those who had not so suffered, 'Cawnpore' was a by-word sufficient to excite the liveliest animosity and the deepest vows of revenge. However true the enunciations of a future under Secretary of State as he moralized over that terrible well, even he, in those early days, might have felt some difficulty in restraining the feeling of vengeance which beset men actively engaged as they thought of one of the most remorseless deeds which ever degraded the nature of man.

Joyous and expectant, therefore, and thirsting for battle, the little force moved from its ground. Cautiously and warily, but with promptitude, the march was conducted till, shortly before dawn, the neighbourhood of the river was reached without opposition. Here the fires of the enemy could be seen extending far to both flanks. The column was halted, and the advanced guard being pushed on, came in collision with a strong outlying picket of the enemy. On discovering the character of the new-comers, however, the latter precipitately retired, and recrossed the river.

Feeling pretty sure that the enemy
had trained his guns to command the
ford and road leading to it, General
Marston halted the main column some
distance short of the river, and left the
enemy to blaze away a few harmless shots
in the belief that he was occupying ground
near the ford. As soon as sufficient daylight enabled him to do so, he rode forward with his staff to inspect the position
of the enemy, and make his arrangements
for attacking him.

The latter occupied the right bank,
where a low range of stony hills rose
somewhat abruptly from the river. His
greatest strength was apparently collected
in the vicinity of the road and ford round

the park of heavy guns. This was evidently considered by him the key of his position. His extreme left rested on a walled village of no great strength, situated amidst cultivated fields, which extended to the base of lofty, jungle-grown hills.

His right wing, still occupying the ridge, was somewhat advanced, owing to the river's slightly bending away from centre to right. This flank might be considered as *en l'air*, it being but slightly protected by a low off-shoot, which ran back for a short distance from the main ridge. Still farther to the right and beyond was an open plain over which were scattered groves of trees and patches of jungle.

So much could the General ascertain from the top of a small hill which was almost opposite the centre of their right wing, and was the most commanding spot in the neighbourhood. This he decided to occupy with his heavy guns, with which he hoped to silence those of the enemy, though so far more numerous. His plan, then, was to attack the right of the position with infantry and a field-battery in conjunction with most of the cavalry and troop of horse artillery, which he determined to send round by a considerable *détour*, with the object of gaining the enemy's right rear. He thus hoped to roll up the rebel right on their centre and left.

The appearance of the cavalry, far

round on the flank, was to be the signal
for his own attack, which was permitted
by the depth of the river—at that point
not exceeding an average of three feet,
except in the pools.

The rebels evidently expected the
English force to endeavour to gain their
side by the high-road through the shallow
ford in front of their centre, and come on
with that bull-dog disregard of all strategy
which has so often distinguished our com-
bats in India. And it became an object,
on the General's part, to keep up this de-
lusion till such time as his preparations
for the real attack were fully completed.

Among the jungle, therefore, near the
bank of the river, at that spot, and in a
line with his own heavy guns, he threw

out a party of English rifle-armed skirmishers with a small support, directing
them to keep up a heavy fire, so as to
mask his movements in their rear. He
then ordered St Clair, with his own regiment, a wing of English hussars, and the
troop of horse-artillery, to make the best
of their way to a ford a mile and a half
lower down. From thence they were to
endeavour, as secretly as possible, to get
on the left and rear of the enemy, while
the General formed his attacking columns
to the left of his heavy gun-battery on
the hill, behind a low ridge which sloped
to the river.

Immediately the enemy perceived that
something was taking place on the hill,
his guns opened on it, besides sending

occasional shots among the skirmishers directly in their front. But the six pieces were got safely into position, and were soon actively returning the somewhat ill-directed rebel fire.

Having seen these movements completed, the General rode further to the left, and brought his light field-battery into play on the rebel right, with the object of replying to some field-pieces there in position. It was, however, directed to throw shell along the whole line, as far as opportunity offered and distance permitted. He then galloped to the extreme left, so as to be clear of the smoke, and reach a position whence he could observe the movements of St Clair and the cavalry. It was not long before he caught an occasional view of them as they threaded their way through some jungle, and the sabres flashed in the rising sun. But unfortunately the enemy on that flank seemed also to have become aware of his movements.

Behind the spur, of which I have spoken as running back from the rebel right, the General and staff could see that they were assembling in force, recruited from other parts of the line, and evidently with guns. They were out of view of St Clair, and might, unless he were warned, take him by surprise.

'Here, Percy! No, Douglas, you, perhaps, had better go. Tell St Clair not to advance into the plain towards that ridge, but endeavour to turn it. Let him

know what they are doing. The moment
I see you near him I will advance the
line and cross the river.'

Galloping to a place lower down, in
obedience to these orders, Douglas crossed
the river and entered on the plain in full
view of the enemy. Shot after shot was
fired in his direction, but he was not in
fair reach, and had accomplished half the
distance unhurt, when, from a small tope
of trees on the left, and near his line, a
mounted picket of the enemy issued, and
galloped so as to cross his front, with the
intention of intercepting him.

They bore on Douglas' left front, and
he sent his horse along at speed, hoping
to get past the point at which they aimed
before they could reach it. But the party,

six or seven in number, were better mounted than he expected, and he soon saw it would be impossible. If he tried to avoid them by inclining to the right, he would be brought directly under fire from the ridge; and on the left—from which direction the picket was galloping —was broken, jungly ground, which would greatly retard his progress—even if he could reach it—and it was imperative to warn St Clair of his danger as quickly as possible. So Douglas decided to hold on, and endeavour to push past or through his assailants.

' May I gallop off with your two orderly troopers to his assistance, sir ? ' asked young Percy of General Marston, as the small knot of officers watched

Douglas' progress.

'It would be useless,' replied the General, though fully alive to the danger his envoy ran. 'Before you could reach him they will be in collision. Douglas is far better mounted than they are, and knows perfectly well what he's about. I hope sincerely he'll manage it somehow.'

'I think he is preparing to attack them single-handed, sir,' observed one of the other officers, watching earnestly through his reconnoitring glass.

'By heaven! yes, it looks like it,' was the reply. 'He can't well avoid them, and won't turn back. It is a case for the cross, if he's successful.'

As the few earnestly and anxiously watched his movements, Douglas had somewhat checked his horse's speed, drawn his revolver from the holster, and loosened his sword in its scabbard. The men, seven in number, had drawn up to oppose him, and were standing in loose open order, so as to present a considerable front, and prevent his passing on either flank.

As he approached all discharged their carbines—with a native's usual eagerness to burn powder—far too soon and without effect, and Douglas replied, when somewhat closer, by firing the barrels of his revolver in rapid succession. One bullet, at least, took effect on one of the horses, as was evident by its falling with its rider.

Trusting now to his sword to defend himself, he made as if to ride at the man overthrown, who was in the centre; then rapidly slightly changing his direction, as he came close, he drove in the spurs and essayed to dash past by the left.   The horseman there, however, was too quick, and made a desperate cut at him.   This Douglas parried, and making a back- handed slash at the trooper as he shot past, had the satisfaction of feeling that his sword had cut deep into the fellow's shoulder.   The next horseman was also close upon him, but wheeled his horse and avoided Douglas' point, and then tried to gallop up and get a cut at him from behind.   The other four were also striving to reach their single adversary before he was fairly past and out of reach.   But the overthrown horse and rider and the fall

of the other wounded man had caused
some slight confusion, and the rest were
never able fairly to overhaul Douglas,
who was now racing away from them at
top speed. Nevertheless they had so far
succeeded as to press him towards the
clump of trees from which they had
issued.

All this was fully seen by the little
band who were watching his proceedings,
and young Percy shouted with excitement
and pleasure as he saw his friend sailing
away, apparently unhurt, beyond his adversaries.

'Most gallantly and excellently
managed,' exclaimed General Marston, as
with grave satisfaction he, too, saw his
emissary emerge from the fray, on the

other side of the enemy. 'Remember, gentlemen, in case anything happens to me to-day, that it. is my intention to re- commend Mr Douglas for the Victoria cross. Now we must advance.' But as the General was turning, an irregular scattered fire was opened from the clump of trees near which Douglas was then passing, and again attracted their at- tention to him. Several foot-soldiers were at the same time seen to advance from their cover, and take deliberate shots at the flying horseman. One of these seemed to take effect, as the latter fell forward on his horse's neck. Quickly recovering himself, however, he waved his sword, as if in contempt or derision at the shout with which the firing party greeted his evident wound, and held on his way.

'I fear the poor fellow is hit,' said the General. 'Trust it's not much. He will reach St Clair now in another minute. Percy, tell Colonel Simpson to advance the line according to the directions I gave him. I shall be with the small column here on the extreme left.'

The different orders were soon carried to the various officers. The line between the heavy guns and the left, which had been keeping up a brisk fire, advanced across the river so soon as they saw the small column referred to brought up and pushed forward.

The rebel fire told severely on both line and column as they crossed; but directly the latter was wheeled and as-

sailed the extreme right flank, and the
skirmishers were called in, the enemy
wavered. Then, as the British appeared
on the hills, the rebels, without waiting to
be charged, broke and retreated towards
the centre and rear. The battery which
had annoyed our centre was soon carried ;
and the roar of the horse artillery, heard
at the same time on the right rear of the
rebel ranks, announced that Douglas'
mission had been successful, and St Clair
enabled to pass well round the enemy's
flank.

All who attempted to escape in that
direction were cut up. Thus far completely
successful, the General now turned his
attention to driving the beaten right back,
with as much loss as possible, and captur-

ing the heavy guns.

He was soon in communication with St Clair, and bringing his infantry round with a sweep, the whole force advanced at nearly right angles to their original position. The captured field-battery of the enemy was turned on the fugitives, and, together with that which accompanied the attacking force, did tremendous execution on the dense masses of the enemy, now completely rolled up and paralyzed and hampered by their very numbers. Some attempted to stand on favourable positions, but were mowed down, and the English force advanced over ground strewn with the dead and wounded.

The fire of the British heavy guns had silenced more than one of the enemy's;

and their shells also created havoc and some panic amongst the massed troops assembled in the centre.

In the plain on the present left of the new line, St Clair had engaged and ridden through the principal cavalry of the enemy, and his sturdy Sikhs and their allies found their arms and swords unequal to the exertion of cutting them down fast enough. At the same time, the wing of Hussars made such effective use of both breech-loading carbine and sword as to cover the ground with dead.

Quarter was little thought of; and the easily-loaded carbine proved a most deadly weapon, when used as a pistol at close quarters.

The heavy guns were next carried.

And, continuing his further advance, the General drove the rebel crowd, now utterly and hopelessly beaten and disorganized, to seek shelter in the village and neighbouring fields.

Here he paused; and re-assembling his men, now considerably scattered, and communicating with the officer in command of the heavy guns before attacking the village, he gave all a rest and time to snatch a hasty meal from the contents of their haversacks.

It was now ascertained that Douglas was indeed hit. He had been struck in the left side by a bullet, but managed to sit his horse and reach St Clair.

After delivering his message, he said to his old and trusty friend, who, indeed, saw from his pallor that something was wrong, 'Hugh, old fellow, I'm hit; badly, I fear. If I don't live to return, tell Helen not to mourn for me. Tell her I love her as of old, now when I believe there is little more time to love in this world. Give me some water. I feel faint.'

St Clair was soon standing on the ground by his wounded friend, and helped to lift him off his horse. Placing him in the shade of a tree, he and the surgeon sought to ascertain the nature of his injuries.

'Cheer up, dear old fellow,' St Clair said as soon as he saw him lying at length in the shade, and refreshed by a draught of water. 'You'll pull through all right.

I am most heartily sorry I can't stay with you. But I'll leave the doctor and a few men, who can join us afterwards. There, good-bye, dear lad, and God bless you, my cherished old friend.' Saying this, the strong, hirsute man, about to engage in deadly strife, stooped down, and with a woman's tenderness pressed a kiss on his friend's forehead as he squeezed his hand. Brothers in heart, words were not needed to assure the stricken man of the deep, commiserating affection of the other— affection so manly in its depth and so womanly in its tenderness. With a glistening eye, but looking far sterner than usual, St Clair galloped to the head of his column, and gave the order to trot.

So soon as the halt was called by the

General, the wounded were collected and brought to the road, and preparations at once made to send them back to the fort under sufficient escort. Every attention was paid them. But there was plenty of work yet to be done, and time did not permit any such lengthened intercourse between friends, sound and wounded, as sentiment might have desired.

Young Percy, however, managed to sit by Douglas for a few minutes—when he with the others was brought up—and endeavoured to cheer him, instead of satisfying a somewhat ravenous young appetite, while Dr Cruickshanks sought to ascertain the nature of the wound and course of the bullet.

The examination concluded, the worthy

doctor shook his head in a melancholy fashion, as he muttered something about 'some sweet oblivious antidote,' and administered an anodyne.

'I thought so, doctor,' said Douglas painfully. 'Better tell me the worst at once. How long do you give me?'

'Ha! hum! We must hope for the best, my dear fellow. But, in fact, the bullet has taken a course which, so to speak—is—hum!—decidedly dangerous, and beyond my ability to reach. "Time is the nurse, and breeder of all good," you know. It may help us.'

'Shall I be able to be carried back to Hussunabad?' asked Douglas.

'No doubt—no doubt,' was the reply. 'If the worst—I only say if—symptoms appear, you would then probably not have more than a few days. But we must hope —we must hope, my good fellow, hope.

"——Walk hence with that,
And manage it against despairing thoughts."'

And the kind-hearted doctor left his patient to attend to others.

'Keep your tail up, dear old fellow,' said Ned Percy, expressing much the same thing, but in language anything but Shakspearian. 'You are to have the cross. The General said so publicly. We were all watching your scrimmage with those "darned critters." It was splendid.'

'The cross!' ejaculated the wounded man, as a faint flush of pleasure lit up his pale face, and his eyes sparkled. 'Very kind of the General. Thank him for me,

Ned. The cross!' he repeated. ' It's worth a limb any day. But a life— Ah, Ned, it's sad to die, or even be invalided, when one is just getting the wind under one's wings, and rising to possible fame and fortune.'

'You'll do that yet,' replied Percy. ' But I must be off; there are the bugles to fall in. Good-bye, dear Douglas. I shall hope to see you all right by the time we return; for of course we shall follow up what gets away of these rascals.'

Affectionately returning the young fellow's greeting, Douglas composed his mind, as well as bodily suffering would allow, to look at the end with equanimity.

Merciful, indeed, is the dispensation which permits a man, in the very hold and grip of death, to view the approaching termination to all that he has struggled for in this world, with less of fear, less of repugnance than he has regarded it from afar.

Meantime, the action, which had been maintained in the brief interval by a few sharp-shooters and field-pieces only, again woke into general vigour.

The heavy guns were moved up the stream, along the bank on which they had hitherto remained, in preference to dragging them through the deep sand and water of the river's bed. From a convenient distance on that side, they shelled and breached the village, where the rebels had posted several heavy guns and a field-battery. These were, for the most part, soon silenced, and preparations were made to carry the village by assault.

St Clair had been detached to watch a road which passed from the village towards the open plain in its rear, and to be prepared to cut up those escaping in that direction. By it, however, the remnants of the enemy's cavalry had already fled with the Rajah ; and already numbers of fugitives could be discerned, making the best of their way up the high, jungly hills I have spoken of.

A field-battery was now moved from battering the village gate-way and placed so as to enfilade the river, and mow down those driven out of the village and seeking to escape by crossing the water, while two columns of attack were formed to enter by the two gates and adjacent broken walls which had been easily breached. The walls were mere shells, more calculated to keep out marauding robbers than cannon-shot. One of the rickety gates had not even been closed, and the other was so shattered by the fire of the field-pieces as to be little of an obstruction.

As the columns advanced a few of the enemy's marksmen—hitherto concealed amongst the fields and low mud-walls—hastily decamped. They were, however, very few, for the bulk of the remaining rebel-force had alrealy evacuated the village, and was in headlong flight. Not quite unopposed, though, did the columns gain possession. Several bands fought

it out to the last, firing with effect from
the principal houses of the village, some
few of which were of two stories, and
towered above the adjacent huts.

Entry into these was forced with difficulty and considerable loss, and, in
one or two instances, the assailants recoiled and sought shelter in the evacuated
dwellings in the neighbourhood. But
these were at last carried, or the house
battered down, and the entire village was
in the possession of the assailants.

After directing St Clair to pursue in
the plain, and detaching a light column of
native infantry—for the European soldiers
were considerably exhausted—to sweep
the fields and dislodge any force of sufficient magnitude which might attempt

to hold any portion of the higher hills, the General withdrew his troops, and took up a position considerably in advance of the village on the Sungumpore road.

Quite satisfied with the crushing defeat he had inflicted on the enemy, and their immense loss, he gave up the rest of the day to recruit his wearied soldiers, and prepare for a further advance towards Sungumpore.

The camp-equipage and baggage— which had been sent for when the action first declared itself in favour of the assailants—was hurried up, and long before evening the camp was pitched and the heavy guns safely parked together with such of those taken as might prove of use in battering the walls of Sungumpore.

The remainder, with those of the wounded who could be transported, were sent back to Hussunabad. Among them Douglas, lying comparatively easy in a hospital dooley, was carried there in safety.

CHAPTER V.

'SAR.   Now, farewell ; one last embrace.
MYR. Embrace, but not the last ; there is one more.
SAR. True, the commingling fire will mix our ashes.
MYR. And pure as is my love to thee, shall they,
Purged from the dross of earth, and earthly passion,
Mix pale with thine.'—*Sardanapalus.*

As dawn fell on fort, city, and camp it roused to the realities and vicissitudes of another day many whose anxiety needed no signal-gun to warn them of its advent. All were early astir, eagerly listening to catch the first intimation of the meeting between friend and foe.

Soon the distant booming of the heavy

guns was distinctly heard, and the auditors were aware that the action had commenced. At first the reverberations were separate and distinct; but these soon became merged in one continuous roll of unceasing sound, varied, however, by the sharper rattle of musketry. To the small force left for the protection of the fort and camp near the cantonments, these sounds were in painful opposition to their own inactive silence. Very hard is it for the true soldier to be defrauded of his share of glory, knowing that, at the distance of a few miles, his comrade is hotly engaged. His own quiescence, quite unavoidable, seems, nevertheless, a slur on his manhood at such a time, and wearies in its very contrast to the excitement of action.

But to loving women's hearts, where professional feeling has no place, it is a time of deep and wearing anxiety. The very indefiniteness of their ideas of battle but serves to increase their fears for the loved ones.

Mrs Atherton and Norah Selby sat together, quiet and subdued, with their thoughts dwelling on the scenes their fancy pictured.

Through the open portals of her imagination, the girl's gaze wandered over a scene dim and undefined, yet possessing a terrible reality in form and incident.

Midst the roar of guns and rattle of musketry—audible facts—she fancied yet the shouts and yells of men meeting in

desperate conflict. Cries in every tone
of agony, passion, hate, triumph, revenge,
despair. And from out of the smoke and
dust of the battle shock, gleamed the
flashes of the cannon, and dimly moved
the actors in the strife. The advancing
lines of infantry, the charge of horse.
Men rushing on, pressing forward, meeting, recoiling, retreating, falling. The
blow, the thrust, the sabre cut, the bayo-
net stab. Wounds, blood, carnage, death.
Hosts of dusky, scowling, turban-crowned
enemies, and friends, so far fewer, but
anger and hate equally animating all.
Men lying on the ground motionless,
others clutching at it in agony, tossing
their arms wildly, reeling and falling.
Fallen horses; others riderless, galloping

to and fro, midst overturned guns and
broken ranks.

All the panoply and wreck of war
mingled in chaotic confusion, as the dim
vision of battle rose before her. But
standing clear and defined rode one loved
figure. Every antagonist seemed to go
down before it. Inspired by a perfect
confidence in its might, she thought none
could withstand the terrible blow of the
brave and stalwart soldier.

With her natural anxiety on behalf
of the loved one, was combined the expectation that he would emerge in safety
from the conflict. Confidence almost
usurped the place of dread.

But far different was it with her companion. She, too, dreamily regarded the

spectral fight, but uncheered with the hopeful confidence which animated the young girl beside her.

She had been deeply impressed with Douglas' supernatural prevision of death. However unwillingly admitted, all potent beliefs and opinions do insensibly sway one deeply interested in the possessor of such.

To feel and believe strongly goes far to affect another in a similar manner. And, in this case, the loving woman more than shared the anticipations of the man she loved.

With action and its excitement, his belief became less of a presence. Other thoughts and ideas occupied his mind. But with her, on the contrary, the flow of life had become stagnant. In her forced inactivity, she dwelt on his anticipation, and made it the guiding principle of her thoughts and fears.

As the day waxed older, rumours of varied import arrived. First there was a whisper—how originated none knew—that our troops had been forced back. Then came a report that they had obtained a partial success. This was followed by contradictory statements respecting our position with regard to the enemy. At last both Mr Selby and the officer left in command received authentic information of the capture of the principal portion of the rebel guns, and that the action was decided in our favour, though with some more work yet to be done.

The loss, on our part, was said to be considerable, but no mention made of individuals.

Thus, for awhile, the poor anxious watchers were left in a state of suspense.

But soon came further news. The rebels were completely beaten with tremendous loss, and the residue in full flight. Our own wounded were being sent in, and the names of several officers, including that of Douglas, were mentioned. St Clair, with the cavalry, it was further announced, was pursuing.

'Dearest Helen,' said Norah, when this report arrived, 'his wound may be slight. We will nurse him till he is well. Come, let us go, and get one of the large tents ready for him.'

Mrs Atherton, without any outward display of emotion, did as her young friend proposed, and both proceeded to make every preparation for the wounded which a woman's thoughtful kindness could suggest.

The long string of dooleys, ambulance carts, and camels with chair frameworks slung on them, was not long in arriving, and the different component parts of the painful procession were guided to the respective quarters assigned them.

Mr Selby had met it, and conducted Douglas to the tent prepared for him. As he reached the spot, Mrs Atherton came out, and looked into the dooley which held Douglas. She was quite composed, for her natural resolution and fortitude, inspired by her most earnest desire to be of help and comfort, had come to her aid, and enabled her to suppress any outward manifestation of anxiety and sorrow.

Douglas smiled faintly as he pressed her hand, and said, ' You see I was right, Helen. But I have come back to you, though for a very short time.'

' Is it a bad wound, dearest Frank ? ' she asked, as dispassionately as she could. ' Norah and I will be such tender nurses. We will soon get you well.'

Douglas shook his head as he said, ' Thanks, dear, and good little Norah, too. She will be glad to know that Hugh St Clair is untouched, and has done splendid service. Now, love, you must retire while

I am moved into the tent.'

He said this, knowing that the pain of removal would be observed by her, and he wished to spare her any needless anguish.

Sad and mournful was that night for many. The 'pride, pomp, and circumstance of glorious war' leave but their shadow to those who mourn for its dead, or watch by the bedside of its wounded victims.

Very many of the ladies exerted themselves womanfully to assist and comfort the sufferers. Regular female nurses there were none; but well did delicately-nurtured ladies supply the want. And foremost amongst them were Norah Selby and Mrs De Silva. Some few there were, indeed, whose nerves or inclinations—

sometimes synonymous terms—prevented
their actual co-operation in the work of
mercy.   But the healthy and healing influence of such is of that negative character that it is best employed by its absence.
Selfishness, or the affectation of fine lady-
ism, is not usually missed by the prostrate
sufferer.   Nevertheless, though Norah was
but slightly imbued with either of these,
it was only by the greatest exertion of
self-control, and the force of her own
sweet, compassionate nature, that she was
enabled to overcome her natural shrinking from the sight of pain, or conquer the
promptings of feminine delicacy and re-
finement.   Encouraged, however, by the
greater experience of her less refined companion, Mrs De Silva, she earnestly and

tenderly prosecuted her determination to be of use.

Many a dull eye gleamed with pleasure, and pale faces lighted up, as the sobered but still bright and cheerful girl paid her visits, and, with the simplicity and tenderness of her nature and sex, inquired after each individual. She never mistook one for another, and each man felt that he was an individual object of genuine interest. Indeed, ere long, she had been made the recipient of an inexhaustible supply of anecdotes of the action, and the full particulars of how and when each man had received his wound.

' Dang it, there she coom!' said John Stodge, one of a knot of men convalescent or slightly wounded, as they sat outside one of the field-hospitals. 'It be as good as a double dram to see her.'

'Hoot! fie, mon!' said Sandy Macgregor, a rough old bearded Scotchman. 'Wad ye be comparing the gude young leddy wi' the likes o' a muckle soop o' speerit? Bless her sonsie face and bonnie bright een, she's mair like a blink o' sunshine on the cauld, misty tap o' a Hielan' hill.'

'Begorra, and that's thrue for you, Sandy, me boy!' Pat Murphy chimed in. 'It's a sperrit she is. But a sperrit of light, so it is. Sure and it's not the dhrink ye would mintion in the same house wid her!'

But whatever the difference of views entertained regarding the appearance of

the young girl, each of the stalwart
speakers stood up and saluted her like an
officer as she approached. Each, too, replied to the pleasant smile and kindly inquiries with which she greeted them, with
a half-bashful, and in the case of the first,
altogether sheepish demonstration of
honest pleasure.

Nor was the presence of kind little
Mrs De Silva unappreciated by those
hairy sons of Mars. She was really of
most practical use as a nurse. But yet
they preferred the less experienced and
imperfectly skilled girl to either her, Mrs
Atherton, or any other. There was a
subtle charm in the simplicity of her
manner, and a pervading essence of guile-
lessness and purity about her which

would have arrested an oath or low expression on the lips of the most abandoned among them.

A soldier, too, as he likes to be commanded by gentlemen, in like manner prefers the attentions of one he regards as a genuine lady of English blood and birth. Thus the good little despised half-caste had much to contend with at first, despite her real use and kindliness. Norah observed this; and always made a point of markedly deferring to her in everything, till at last the men themselves came insensibly to recognize her real merits as a nurse.

But the greater part of Mrs Atherton's time was occupied with Douglas. The ball could not be reached, and the doctors were soon obliged to confess that the case was hopeless.

Douglas was perfectly prepared for this announcement. He had, from the first, felt that his wound was mortal. But to Mrs Atherton, not unexpected though it was, it came as a heavy blow. She sorrowed with an exceeding bitter sorrow. The light and charm of existence seemed about to be taken from her little personal world, and henceforth it must be passed in the gloom and shadow of perpetual night. She had greatly altered in mind and the bearings of her character in these few years, and she now felt that with his death the chance of happiness on which she had cast her all must turn up a blank.

But she strove with all her force to

conceal it from him, and to soothe his last hours with the ministering tenderness of a loving woman.

And in the close intimacy of an affection sweeter than friendship, he talked to her now more freely than he had ever done. He told her of the perfect regeneration of his love, and of his hopes that in the world of spirits, to which he was hastening, they might hereafter meet divested of all the coarser emotions attaching to our mortal frames. He dwelt on the communion of spirit in realms from which was banished all that savoured of earth, earthy; where the unshackled essence, cleansed of its human clog, and freed from all the demands of an artificial society, should rise triumphant, and soul cleave to soul in the perfect purity of a hallowed affection. With the self-control she had resolved to exercise, as women sometimes can, she frequently sang to him his favourite song —that beautiful wail of a departing spirit —Schubert's 'L'Addio.'

Then he talked to her of his little sister, of his pretty Lilly, just blossoming in her spring. And she faithfully promised to be indeed a sister to the child, and love her for the sake of the one whose memory would be so dear to both.

Of the old governor, too, in the pretty country home on the banks of the rushing trout-stream, where yet the old man wielded a not unskilful fishing-rod, he made frequent and affectionate mention.

She encouraged him to talk of old familiar faces and scenes, and they now in these last days,

'Came back to him with recollected music.'

He described the very spot, and all the circumstances attending the capture of his first trout. Ah, how everything connected with thát important event stood out in full relief. He recalled to mind the rushing river just below the old, one-arched, stone bridge, the broken dyke, and the fir plantation on the opposite side of the stream, with the rough heather-covered hill behind. The bed of shingle he stood on, and on which the captured fish—weighing about two ounces—was safely landed, to his inexpressible delight —a delight too ecstatic for words. Then

he remembered his father's cheerful congratulations, his mother's pride, and the
excitement of the whole household at
master Frank's success.   How very much
of a hero he felt himself for the next
twenty-four hours!   Ay, even in the
early summer morning, long before the
hour of rising, when he awoke and got
up to inspect his trophy, which he had
surreptitiously carried to his bed-room
the night before.   He remembered how
this was subsequently discovered by his
old nurse, and the offence condoned by
much affectionate conduct on his part.

Then came the sad episode of his
mother's death.

All the little incidents of his child
life, some, till now, almost forgotten, as-

sumed a distinctness and vividness which was generally absent from far more recent events. On these he lovingly dwelt, and she tenderly sympathized with him as she listened.

And on one occasion he told her something of that tale of woman's sin and sorrow, to which former reference has been made, alluding to her as 'Mary.'

Ever and anon, too, he would recur to the happiness he hoped was in store for his old friend, St Clair; and he told her more fully of the advantage which he had derived from his society and friendship. Of Norah he spoke, and sometimes to, in terms of affectionate and admiring interest, fully believing that she would make his dear friend a good and loving wife.

Ned Percy also came in for a full share of his remembrances. To each of his friends he left some trifling little memorial. A little trinket or book, or sporting accessary, such as a powder-flask or fishing-rod, which has all the value of a costly present to loving natures,—and such only had he to leave. All his more valuable possessions he knew would be required to meet his debts.

And foremost among recent occur-rences, he talked of the intention of Gene-ral Marston to recommend him for the Victoria cross. Percy's intimation had been confirmed in a very kind and sympa-thizing letter from the General, which Mrs

Atherton read to her patient every day. Although he knew he could not live to receive it, the fact was none the less cheering, and he pictured to himself the pride with which the news would be learnt at home,—some compensation, he trusted, for the tidings which must so soon follow when the old man and the young girl would be left desolate.

He managed to write to each a few lines of loving greeting, bidding them not sorrow for him. And in the longer note to his sister, he referred to his sentiments as death approached. He touched in a brave and manly way on his sense of the mercy of One who knew his mortal frailty, who was perfectly acquainted with what had been his temptations, and to whom all his most hidden sins and weaknesses were clear as light, and in Him he rested his trust that they might be forgiven.

He wrote, too, of his darling Helen, commending her to his sister's love as one who in happier circumstances might have been her relative indeed. He told his sister what a comfort she was to him, how she soothed him, and read to him, and prayed for and with him; and he enclosed letters from the General, St Clair, and Percy, and especially referred to the two latter as his dearest friends.

Having arranged his affairs as best he could, and thus prepared himself and others, he calmly awaited the now fast approaching end.

But his constitution was strong, and wrestled fiercely, always beaten, yet always only reluctantly relinquishing its ground, as the advancing strides of death subdued it.

One morning before dawn he awoke from a feverish slumber, strangely free from pain, and when Mrs Atherton paid him her early morning visit, she saw that in his face which too surely announced the close approach of the last sad scene.

The doctor only confirmed this on his arrival, and indicated the cause of the comparative freedom from pain.

Douglas himself well knew what it portended, and the surgeon had no hesitation in avowing that his very hours were numbered.

The sick man requested that the side door of the tent towards the rising sun might be opened, so as to give him a clear uninterrupted view. The sun rose in all the gorgeous magnificence of the eastern clime it shone on, infinitely more brilliant, but far less beautiful, than in more temperate regions. With his Helen's hand clasped in his own right one—the left was powerless—the dying soldier looked on the last sun which was to gild the days of his earthly pilgrimage.

'It is the last I shall see, Helen, dearest,' he whispered in a weak, low voice. And then added, looking fondly at her, 'What should I have done without you? You mustn't regret me very much. Stoop, love, and kiss me.'

She did so without speaking, and then whispered in his ear a little favourite prayer of his which she had learnt by heart. He pressed her hand as she concluded, and then she moistened his parched lips with some cooling beverage which stood ready on a table close at hand.

'Put—arm—round—neck,' he next said.

This she did, and knelt by the low couch, so as to render the position easier for both, and supported his head on her shoulder.

' Remember, Ned, and Hugh St Clair, governor, sister, all. I could fancy I see my mother and poor Mary. Ah, poor, poor girl ! It wasn't her fault. God pity her, and have mercy on us all.'

The speaker paused, and lay back silent, as if exhausted, for a considerable time. Suddenly, however, he started up, and in accents far louder than might have been expected from his previous indications of weakness, exclaimed,

'Hurrah! victory! The cross! Lilly —Helen—Peace—'

His head fell back, still encircled by her loving arm, and as she bent over him she kissed, with the calmness of despair, all that remained to her of Frank Douglas.

CHAPTER VI.

' Unbarr'd, unlock'd, unwatch'd, a port
Led to the castle's inner court :
There the main fortress, broad and tall,
Spread its long range of bower and hall,
And towers of varied size.'

The Bridal of Triermain.

LET us now return to General Marston and his little army.

St Clair rejoined the camp late on the night of the action, having cut up many bands of fugitives, and dispersed others, thus preventing any general re-assembling of the defeated force in the vicinity of the British camp.

Early on the following morning the General moved forward,' and learning from his spies and the villagers that the Rajah and the whole of those who had escaped were making for Sungumpore, he pushed on toward that place by forced marches.

On the morning of the seventh day he appeared before Sungumpore, and, escorted by the whole of his cavalry, reconnoitred the entire place.

That it was to be defended was evident. Indeed, a round shot or two tossing up the dust as it came ricochetting towards them, announced that, though the party was not within fair range, the enemy took cognizance of its movements, and sent a cartel of defiance.

Well pleased were all to find that a stand was to be made. The reports of the Rajah's amazing wealth had circulated with that magnifying power which usually attends large possessions even in the western world.

Bricks of gold and blocks of silver in incalculable numbers, and jewels of untold value, were said to be stowed away in the palace. Loot, such abundant loot as it hardly entered into the heart of man to conceive, was predicted. The Rajah's determination to fight it out in his stronghold clearly indicated to the contemplative mind that he found it impossible to move or desert his cherished treasure. And as on this subject every mind in the force was contemplative, the determination was welcomed with unmixed satisfaction, signifying, as it did, that nothing but a little hard fighting was required to transfer possession of the accumulated hoards.

General Marston determined to assault the place with as little delay as possible, and thus take advantage of the dejection caused by the defeat the enemy had already sustained.

But the place was large, and his little force far too small to invest it. The town extended for a length little short of a mile on the banks of a deep river, fully three hundred yards across, and passable only by boat. On the land side an un-interrupted line of massive-built bastions and curtains reaching from one part of the river to another, gave the place a name for strength which it well deserved. But it was the palace in which had culminated all the resources of the native engineer. This was a large block of buildings fortified in itself, and might be said to form the citadel of the whole place. If the town were taken, this would still remain to be carried. It occupied entirely one end of the town, and was the only part with regular defences on the river bank. Here a mighty piece of masonry, called the water-bastion, upwards of a hundred feet in height, domineered over city, river, and country. The city was further protected on one side by a lake, which washed the walls, and helped to supply the moat with water.

A brief examination decided the General to concentrate all his power of attack on the citadel itself. No doubt if the town were first carried, the stronghold would be found' more vulnerable on its town side. But he preferred trusting to a single assault, for if the citadel fell,'the whole place would follow, as a matter of course.

With this object he selected as his position a low ridge which abutted on the river, the latter serving as a protection to his left.

During the night rough breaching-batteries were thrown up in advance of the position, without any attempt at sapping, and in the morning he made efforts to feel the enemy's strength in artillery.

It was soon ascertained that in that respect he was weak. Evil for him had been the day when he so ill-advisedly risked in the open his cherished guns, some of which were now thundering against him. Still he had mounted enough of tolerably heavy guns to give some trouble at long range. And these were supplemented by a number of small wall pieces and ginghals, which at close quarters might prove very destructive.

A desultory fire was kept up during the day, and an occasional shell pitched into the citadel. But no regular bombardment was commenced. Some of the engineer officers, and those of the Quartermaster General's department, made more than one reconnoitring excursion with the object of ascertaining the most vulnerable point of attack. They possessed no regular plan of the place ; but a native sketch, wonderfully out of drawing, gave them some faint conception of the defences and interior.

Towards evening, one of the reconnoitrers discovered what he thought might prove a weak point. He observed that a portion of one of the curtains looked newer than the rest, and the idea was suggested that probably some crack in the wall, or flaw, had been hastily and imperfectly repaired. A shot or two was directed on this point, and the crumbling masonry gave indications that the surmise was probably just.

On this, then, it was decided to con-

centrate the fire at daylight on the following morning, by which time the General
hoped to have all the heavy guns in position, as well as some field-pieces, and a
battery of small mountain mortars. Rifle-
pits and mounds were also directed to be
made so as to cover a few selected shots,
to pick off the enemy's artillerymen, or
anything showing itself on the ramparts.

Hopeful and buoyant, officers assembled
at their various messes that evening in the
rough-and-ready campaign fashion. Pro-
digious *shaves* were afloat concerning the
magnitude of the expected loot; and
young Percy entered on the subject in the
staff mess-tent, after dinner that night,
on the General's retirement; Dr Cruickshanks, and a friend of his own only,

however, being present to benefit by his ideas.

'They say the " swag " will be something tremendous,' he observed. ' There is a report that in some underground place there are regular stacks of diamonds and emeralds.   It makes one feel quite solemn to think of it.'

> ' The gravity and stillness of your youth
> The world hath noted,'

said Dr Cruickshanks.

' Very correct and proper of the world, indeed,' was the reply. ' I shouldn't have given it credit for such discrimination. But then, you see, I judge by those about me, and I greatly fear *they* have not properly appreciated my many excellencies.'

' No,' returned the doctor. ' You have,

Ned, a remarkably modest way about you of concealing them. I would hardly accuse you of hiding your light under a bushel; but somehow those excellencies you speak of have escaped observation.'

'Sorry for you, doctor. Your want of discernment is no fault of mine. I know I'm very modest, but my excellencies are apparent enough. I'm afraid your contracted understanding is in fault.'

'It would certainly take a wonderful understanding to discover your perfections. They are like the philosopher's stone, Ned, always sought for and never found.'

'Bad metaphor, doctor. Better say they are like a pair of spectacles, which some old fellow has raised to his forehead, and searches for everywhere. They are right before him, if he only had the 'cuteness to find them. But it's only very clever people who understand me.'

This last was spoken with an assumption of the greatest seriousness, which was, however, changed as Mr Percy turned to his guest at mess, and said, as he looked at his watch,

'Time drawing on, Stanford.'

'Gad! yes, half-past nine, so it is,' returned the individual addressed.

'Time for what?' asked Dr Cruickshanks.

'Oh, only a little business we have got in hand. Like to join us, doctor? We are going on a voyage of discovery.'

'Why, thank you, no. Any voyage of

discovery originated by you might lead to

" The undiscover'd country from whose bourne
No traveller returns."

Pray hold me excused. I have more respect for a sound skin than to join you. But what mischief are you up to to-night ? '

' Well, I heard the General say he wished he had a few more boats. So we are going to pull quietly down in one of those we got hold of yesterday, and see if we can't manage to tow up a lot of those lying off the steps under the palace. Cartwright and Seely of the Highlanders are coming. They are both good oars, and Stanford also joins.'

' Now, I hope you boys are not going to do anything so foolish,' the doctor replied anxiously. ' I'm sure, Ned, the General wouldn't approve of it, and as for St Clair— By Jove, I'll go and look him up!'

'Then you'll have to bestride that thunderbolt of yours without any moon to pluck honour from or light you on the way. It's a queer country in the dark, away on the right; and St Clair was to visit the pickets, and patrol there at nine.'

'Well, but, you foolish madcap, I really am anxious about this proposed freak. You don't really mean anything of the sort, Stanford?'

' Oh no, doctor. It's all Percy's chaff. We only talked of a quiet little pull on the river. Up, not down.'

' Take care what you do,' replied the

doctor, but partially satisfied with this explanation. 'However, I'm off to roost.

"Good night, good night! parting is such sweet sorrow."'

'Ah, yes. Leave us a lock of your hair, doctor,' said Percy.

'Not I,' was the rejoinder. 'You would send it to some pretty girl as your own.'

'Your hair! A pretty one!' exclaimed Percy. 'Venus forbid.'

'Wouldn't trust you; but I'm off, and advise you boys to follow my example. I only hope that "villainous saltpetre" will not disturb my rest.'

Notwithstanding Mr Stanford's assertion, the excursion referred to had been actually planned and proposed by Ned

Percy. To carry it into effect he had sought and readily obtained the aid of three congenial spirits, whose aptitude for a lark, generally devil-may-care dispositions, and singular deficiency in what ordinary people call 'nerves,' rendered them fitting allies. Stanford had dined with him. The other two were to meet at his tent at 10 o'clock. They would have made it later, but the moon's rising about midnight prevented its postponement.

'Wish we had poor old Douglas with us,' said Percy to his assembled friends, as they 'liquored up'—to use the speaker's mode of expressing it—before starting on their expedition. 'It would have been such a nice sort of little trip

for him. How he would enjoy it, and
then he's got such a good head for these
affairs. I'm afraid the poor old fellow is
not likely to last to enjoy many more in
this line.' And the young fellow sighed
with a genuine feeling of deep commiser-
ation as he thought of his friend's state,
as last reported, and compared it with
his own present vigour, and the prospect
of employing it in the forthcoming adventure.

However, there was no time to be lost;
so the party of four walked down to that
part of the river where the boat referred
to was moored. Percy had made all his
arrangements with a foresight hardly to
have been expected from him. As they
dropped quietly down with the current,

close to the bank, his whispered countersign passed him, without inquiry, at the
guards and pickets situated on the river's
bank, and they were soon beyond these.

All was quiet, or seemed so. Ammunition was too precious in the English
camp to waste in night firing; and apparently the garrison of the fort had not
yet discovered the proceedings of the
working-parties, or attempted to inter-
rupt them.

Black and supernaturally large, some
of the more mighty bastions stood out as
the rowers dropped quietly towards them.
No lights glanced across them, and, save
for some illuminated windows of the interior buildings of the palace, and an
occasional challenge, there appeared few

indications of active life within the grim and sombre fortress. The further bank of the river loomed indistinctly, checkered by groups of trees, whose irregular form broke the sky-line.

Bold as were the four young fellows, their heart-beats somewhat quickened as they noiselessly crept beneath the frowning bastion which connected the river-defence with the landward line of works. Unsuspicious of danger from that quarter, however, no sentry seemed to be posted to keep watch and ward over the river; and unchallenged they passed on.

Immediately beyond this existed a considerable space of rough, rocky, open ground, lying between the river and the wall which connected the bastion just mentioned and the huge structure that I have previously referred to. This was used as a general bathing-place, and thence, too, water was drawn for the garrison. About midway between the two bastions was the landing-place; and well-built steps led thence to the postern-gate in the wall, which there gave entrance to the palace. At the foot of the steps the boats were moored.

These, too, were reached in safety by the adventurous little exploring party, and they proceeded to select two or three capacious boats, and attach them to their own small craft with ropes provided for the purpose.

This operation effected, it occurred to the enterprising Mr Percy that they

might as well explore the neighbourhood,
and ascertain what sort of gate it was,
which, at the distance of some fifty yards,
stood on the top of the steps. He argued
that knowledge on this subject could
not be hurtful, and the enemy were so
kindly inattentive to their proceedings
that it were pity their courtesy should be
thrown away.

Leaving the other two, therefore, in
the boat all ready to pull out into the
stream, Percy and Stanford proceeded on
their little tour of inspection. They soon
reached the top of the steps, and found
that a small wicket let into the massive
frame of the large gate was actually ajar.

Gently opening it, Percy cautiously
peered in. Beyond appeared what seemed

to be a flight of steps rising up through the thick walls, and opening on to the terre-plein above. So much, at least, he judged from seeing the open sky at the top of the steps.

Observing no signs of the enemy's presence, or any sufficient reason why he should not prosecute his researches still further, he thought he might as well introduce his body after his head; so he noiselessly stepped through the aperture, followed by his companion.

They silently ascended without let or hindrance, but with hands ready to their revolvers, and prepared to turn and run for it on the first appearance of an enemy.

None such appeared; and they were

just about to step out on the open ground above, when the sound of voices close at hand arrested them.

The speakers were evidently stationary, so Percy protruded his head with the object of ascertaining if it were a guard or some casual party of men straying there. Very little could he make out. He saw, however, two or three figures which, even as he looked, walked away in an opposite direction. His first impulse on hearing voices had been at once to bolt; but now his confidence was restored, and he saw no reason to forego further inquiries into the state of affairs in his immediate vicinity.

'The coons seem dormant,' he whispered into Stanford's ear. 'Vote we take advantage of it.'

'I'm game, go ahead,' was the curt rejoinder. So go ahead Mr Percy did, but warily, and keeping a keen look-out around. So keen, indeed, were his peerings into the darkened void on either hand, that he unfortunately neglected to observe a few bundles of things at his very feet.

The first intimation he had of the presence of such, was very nearly falling prostrate over one of the said bundles, which, with dire anathemas, in the choicest Hindustanee, resented this intrusion on its slumbers. In fact, Mr Percy had literally, as well as metaphorically, stumbled on the guard, or at least a portion of it, which was 'taking its rest with its martial cloak around it.'

'Least said soonest mended,' occurred to the intruder, as he suppressed the half-muttered 'd—n' which rose to his lips. But the recumbent figure thought it necessary to rise to a sitting posture, and make—to Percy—some incoherent inquiries as to the reason for being thus disturbed. To this was appended several choice epithets of abuse which the listener did chance to understand, as being the common native mode of expressing sentiments of displeasure.

Without a word Percy retreated, and the somnolent sentry rose to his feet, doubtful as to his impression of having seen the pale face of an Englishman. He called out, however, after the quickly retiring figures, which he discerned silently disappearing in speediest fashion into the aperture which led to the gate. He saw something was wrong, and, after again shouting to the intruders, fired his piece into the air.

Immediately thereon a quick interchange of question and answer rang out from the nearer bastions, and the sharp rattle of arms sounded unpleasantly close to the fugitives, as the sleeping guards started into activity.

Down the steps the two went as fast as their active limbs could carry them, and then they plunged headlong through the gate-way, and continued their rapid course down to the boats.

By the time these were reached, that

part of the garrison which had been taking its rest on the ramparts overlooking them was fully alive to the fact that something unusual was in course of perpetration below. They were evidently preparing to use their guns, as the four explorers could learn by the noise which attended their loading.

Percy and Stanford jumped hastily into the small boat in which their comrades were seated, and all manfully pushed and pulled, till they found themselves afloat and moving out into the stream. Here, however, they were checked by the rope which had been attached to the pilfered boats, and Seely sung out to Percy, who was pulling the stroke-oar or paddle, to cut the rope and let the boats go.

'Haven't got a knife,' was the reply.
'Never mind. Pull away. They'll think
the big boats are full of men, and will
blaze away at them.'

It was hard work. But manfully they
strove to gain the opposite bank. As for
passing close in under the bastion, as
they had come, such a thing was not now
to be thought of. 'Distance lent' decided 'enchantment to the view' at present.

The rattle of musketry was soon succeeded by the roar of a wall-piece, and
the shot plunged into the water far a-head
of them.

'Keep out of that line. Pull more to
the right,' shouted Percy. 'It will take a

good shot to hit us in the dark.'

They were soon beyond much danger from musketry ; but three or four guns were now opened on them and in full activity. Shot after shot struck about them, tossing up the water in high jets, but now mostly astern. Probably, as Percy had conjectured, what little aim the enemy could take, according to the sound of the oars, or by observing their position from the flash of the previous gun, was made with the object of hitting the large boats.

Even by daylight, and in a position more adapted for good aiming, it is not every bullet, which ' has its billet.' Indeed, the fire of round-shot is to human life, ordinarily, the most indestructive mode of applying gunpowder. The tons of iron which could be sent hurtling through the air, without much loss to life, is amazing. I speak of times when there was hardly an 'Armstrong' in India, and anterior to the advent of great rifled ordnance.

Wide and harmless, therefore, as yet fell the shot, and the rowers, exerting all their energies, were making fair way, notwithstanding their now undesired tail.

Still untouched, they drew close to the opposite shore, and, in a few jerky sentences, held council of war. This was briefer and more decisive than usually follows the consultations of those who, in military matters, believe that 'in the multitude of counsellors there is wisdom.'

'Let's land and cut for it till we get opposite camp, and there shout for a boat,' suggested Cartwright, who was pulling in the bow.

'Better untackle our tow, and make the best of our way in the boat,' observed Seely.

'I second you, Seely,' said Stanford. 'We shall catch it for losing one of the only two boats. Vote we stick to it.'

'Pull away, and don't lose time in jawing,' said Percy, as he gave a vigorous tug at his paddle, serving to turn the boat's head up-stream. 'I'm stroke-oar and captain. Hanged if I'll desert our prizes, since we've got them so far ! '

To this none objected. The speaker spoke authoritatively and decisively, and, as is usual, carried his hearers with him.

On they toiled, still presenting a target for the night-practice of the fort guns, which, however, became wilder and wilder. But soon a new danger presented itself.

The garrison, taken by surprise and not knowing in what force were the invaders on their domain, had at first contented themselves with firing from the bastions and ramparts. But it now became evident that men were assembling at the landing-place, and, perhaps, preparing to embark with the object of intercepting the fugitives.

'Pull like blazes,' ejaculated Percy, who had an eye like a hawk, and kept a good look-out about him. 'I do believe they are going to give chase. I suppose I must cast off these spoils of ours. Any body got a knife?' he asked, as he tugged ineffectually at the knot by which the rope was fastened.

No one had. And Ned Percy returned to his oar, as he said, 'Well! there's no help for it now. The knot's jammed; I tugged at it with my teeth, till I feel as if I had cracked my jaw, and had dined on tar. Now a hearty pull, Shabash! she would move beautifully if we only had her alone.'

The struggling fugitives were now in mid-stream, and about three hundred yards above the outer bastion of the palace. Three or four boats, full of the enemy's troops, could be discerned on the deep leaden line of the water pulling closer in shore, in the hope of intercepting the Englishmen before they reached their advanced pickets, and in this there was every probability of their succeeding.

Even Percy and Stanford, the two boldest, began to think the case looked awkward, when the rattle of small arms and a stentorian voice was heard on the river bank.

'Who goes there? Stop, I till ye, and spake the worrd in dacent Inglish or Oirish, which is the same, or I'll shot ye.'

'Hurrah!' shouted Percy, 'we are friends. I'm Mr Percy, the General's aide-de-camp, and some other officers. I'll come and give the countersign, only look out below there. .There are a lot of boats full of niggers. Blaze away at them. They are chasing us.'

'Sure an that's thrue for you, yer honour. It's meself that's seeing them. Sergeant, here's a power of naigur black fellers a-chasing the Giniral's aide. Will I fire upon them?'

The pursuing boats paused as they heard this brief colloquy. Fortunately for Mr Percy and his companions a patrolling party had been pushed forward with the object of endeavouring to ascertain the cause of the firing going on from the water-bastions.

'Canny, my mon,' said another voice, as the sergeant drew up his party all ready for the reception of the boats alluded to.

'Ye suldna be in siccan a hurry.   If yon's
the naigers, I'll gie it em.   But we maun
ascerteen preccesely wha' they are.'

Saying this, he roared out in broadest
Scotch, requesting to be informed who
and what they were, and if friends to advance and deliver the countersign.   But,
by this time, the pursuers evidently considered that they had come far enough,
and that a retrograde movement was desirable.   This was observed by the party on
the bank.

'Faik! sergeant, it's naigurs they are.
There's no doubt at all, at all.   Will I fire
before they slip away?'

'Fire and be d—d till them,' the sergeant replied with native vigour.   'Naigurs they maun be, nae doot aboot it.

Noo, my men, tak' it aisy. Aim as weel
as ye can, and fire low, by files from right.
Ready ! '

To the great delight of Percy and his
comrades, who were now pulling in towards the party on the bank, a brisk fire
was kept up on the retreating boats till
they got out of reach behind the bastion.

' A narrow squeak that, sergeant,' said
Percy, as he gave the pass, and satisfied
that astute non-commissioned as to who he
was. ' I don't know how you fellows feel,'
he said, turning to his companions. ' I'm
pretty nearly done. Let's have a suck at
the monkey. Stanford, you've got it,
haven't you ? '

Stanford had got the monkey, and
produced it in the shape of a large flask ;

and as the rest of the party were, equally with their captain, exhausted by their hard pull, the monkey was sucked nearly dry.

'It wad be them boats ye were crib-bing, sir?' said the sergeant, interroga-tively, as he pointed to those hardly-won vessels; 'an' that led to the firing?'

'Quite right,' was the reply. 'Hope there hasn't been much of a row in camp in consequence?'

'Dinna ken, sir. I was on picket, and was thrown forward by the captain to speer what a' the firing was aboot. Might I mak sae boold as to inquire if ye went richt to the fort?'

'Clean into it by an open gate,' was the reply. 'Tumbled over the guard, and was chased, as you saw. However, we've got what we went for.'

'Begorra! They are the rale stuff.' ''A domned bowld thing, as ever I heerd tell on.' These and such like exclamations, made *sotto voce* by the men, showed the marked approval with which those lowly warriors of the ranks heard of the exploit.

'An richt weel pleased am I, sir,' said the sergeant, 'that ye and the other gentlemen are standing there weel and fut. 'Deed, it was an unco' venturesome—'

Just then, however, the sergeant's eloquence was interrupted by the flash and roar of a gun from the nearest bastion, and the singing of a round shot overhead was heard, as it rushed through the night-air.

The officer commanding the picket, too, made his appearance, and, on hearing the particulars, withdrew his men. At the same time Percy and his comrades once more betook themselves to their oars, and safely towed their prizes to the camp.

CHAPTER VII.

' K. HEN. Once more unto the breach, dear friends,
  once more ;
Or close the wall up with our English dead.'
                              King Henry the Fifth.

GENERAL MARSTON learnt next morning of his aide-de-camp's escapade· with
feelings of no little wonder, and some admiration. These, however, he dissembled,
and Mr Percy had to submit to what he
called a ' rattling good whigging.'

Having relieved his mind of its sense
of duty by the administration of said
whigging, however, the General made

more particular inquiries into the details of the adventure, in which he really took great interest. And when he walked down to the river, and inspected the three really good and serviceable boats, which were the fruits of the expedition, he spoke no more in tones of reproof.

Indeed, in conversation with the senior engineer officer, and other elders of the force, he expressed his unqualified admiration for the pluck and determination with which the affair had been conducted. And it was observed afterwards that the comrades of Mr Percy in that affair became not infrequent guests of the General.

In the mean time the boats were cheaply purchased by the commotion among the pickets and covering parties,

to which the unaccountable firing attending their capture had given rise.

But Ned Percy principally wondered
what the 'old man' would say to his exploit; and was greatly gratified when he
found that said 'old man' was hugely de-
lighted at his young relative's courage
and resolution. Moreover, as one of his
subalterns had been wounded in the action at Nuddipore, he applied for Ensign
Stanford to fill the temporary vacancy,
which application was successful, to the
great content both of that officer and his
friend Percy.

It would be tedious to relate to the
non-professional reader each day's progress in the siege. Let it suffice to say
that the curtain selected proved to be

the weak point in the defences, and very soon exhibited signs of shortly becoming a practicable breach.

A continued fire was kept on it, and the General made his preparations for assaulting the place, whenever it should be reported assailable. Another spot was also selected for breaching, both with the object of dividing the attention of the enemy, and also of enabling the General.to deliver his attack in two separate columns.

But it was the main breach in the weak curtain on which he principally relied to give him entrance.

His superiority in heavy artillery had enabled him a good deal to keep down the enemy's fire, so that his loss hitherto had been comparatively small. Full of heart, therefore, and eager to come to close quarters, the besiegers received orders one evening to prepare for the assault on the following morning.

A heavy fire was kept up all night, and a shell thrown every few minutes served to keep alive the attention. of the enemy, and caused several explosions of small magazines. About a couple of hours before dawn the whole force got under arms, and the columns of attack were told off.

These consisted of two assaulting parties of 500 men each, half of English, half of native infantry, supported by a reserve of 700. A smaller detachment was detailed to occupy both banks of the river, and intercept fugitives by

water. For this purpose ' Percy's craft,'
as the little fleet had been christened, together with some rafts constructed by the
engineers, came into use.

St Clair, with the cavalry, was detailed
to watch the two principal gates of the
town, and act on such bodies of the
enemy as might seek flight by them.
But he was directed to hold his force
together, only keeping up a constant
patrol between the two gates, which were
widely separate, and make every endeavour to capture any of the leaders
who might escape.

The seizure of the third gate, which
led into the citadel from the land
side, was to be the principal object of the
first attacking column after it had forced

entrance by the breach. By this the General hoped to give entry to his reserve, thus brought up and launched on the enemy fresh and unattacked.

The second assaulting column was to make a feint on the second breach. This feint, however, was to be converted into a real assault if circumstances were propitious, or the breach easy. Otherwise, after effecting its object of dividing the attention of the defenders, it was to push along to the assistance of the first assaulting column.

By the time the morning star, herald of the sun, rose in the east, the columns of attack were collected in and about the advanced batteries and trenches, all prepared for the signal rocket which was to launch them on their errand of slaughter.

General Marston, with his staff, had established his head-quarters in a small battery of field-pieces which had been pushed forward to within a short distance of the enemy's walls. This was even now engaged in sweeping the face of the breaches, and keeping clear the way to them.

• Dawn, impatiently looked for by many whose eyes were never destined to see another, at length tardily lightened the horizon. The first faint streaks of white grew rapidly into broader mass, and the time had arrived when there existed suffi-cient light for the columns to find their way, and take advantage of the cool, invigorating freshness of the early morn.

The rocket which shot into the air was paled by the quickly increasing light, but still sufficiently obvious to those alert and watching for its appearance.

Immediately it was fired the two columns advanced, preceded a short distance by the leading companies, and engineers with ladders, which. formed the forlorn hopes. Steadily they moved on, regardless of the shot which struck in and about them, and left no few marks of its destructiveness. When within a short distance, with a wild hurrah the forlorn hope of the first column rushed forwards, and quickly descending into the dry moat—half filled with the *debris* of the battered walls— sought to ascend the breach. Here a destructive musketry fire was poured in on them, and the head of the column recoiled. Quickly recovering, however, the men again pressed forward, encouraged by wild shouts from the rear, exhorting them to renewed exertion, or the other column would beat them and be first in.

A party of sharp-shooters also, judiciously left on the brink of the moat, kept up so well-directed and sustained a fire into the very throat of the breach, as soon to clear it of its defenders, who sought the more protected shelter of the parapets on either side.

Led by young Seely—for the captain of the company had been shot down—the forlorn hope toiled manfully over the stones, and earth, and mortar which, in disjointed masses, formed their uncertain foothold. Struggling on, they reached the top of the slope, but were there brought to a stand by finding a rough, hastily-made palisade of wooden branches of trees, stumps, and anything which had been available. But not for long were they checked. A sergeant soon found an assailable part where a recent round shot had torn its way rending and weakening the obstruction. There seemed, too, to be a sudden pause in the direct fire from above, so that some by this gap, others by ladders, forced their way, and were now rapidly assembling on the parapet. An entrance was won, and, amidst the smoke, the General had soon the satisfaction of catching a momentary glimpse of the

British colours planted at the top of the breach, as the now risen sun gleamed upon them.

The firing was soon recommenced, and continued severe and sharp. The progress of the column could be discerned by the roll of musketry, as it slowly made its way towards the gate it had been directed to seize from within.

Just then a part of the breach and parapet about it was seen to heave, and the riven masonry separate in large masses. To this succeeded a bright light, breaking into numberless radiating forks and tongues; a discharge into air of stones and earth and dead bodies; a thick, black smoke, which slowly curled, twisting and writhing, into the upper air;

a trembling of the earth, and then a crash. A mine had been sprung, but fortunately too late to do much injury to other than the dead, who lay on the upper part of the breach.

An almost breathless silence seemed momentarily to follow the convulsion of earth and air. But it was of short duration, and all the sounds of desperate conflict were renewed.

But with the failure of the explosion the enemy lost heart, and in the confusion succeeding, the second attack also managed to effect a footing on the ramparts by escalade.

'Now, gentlemen,' said the General to his staff, 'we will call for our horses and enter the fort with the reserve. All is going on even more satisfactorily than I could have anticipated.'

They soon joined the reserve, which was now directed to march on the gate near which the firing indicated the continued lateral advance of the first column.

But, although some stand was made there, the enemy was forced back, and the double gates, one at either end of the way which wound round a massive bastion, were opened, or battered down. The reserve then entered, and proceeded to join in the attack.

Before the General entered he despatched one of his staff to inform St Clair of their successful assault, and the probability that the enemy would shortly endeavour to escape from the gates of the town, or be driven to do so by our advance into it.

Along the narrow street which led to the heart of the numerous straggling buildings forming, in their entirety, the palace and its precincts, the column forced its way. Opposition there was, and several buildings, from whence issued a destructive fire, had to be carried by direct assault. The bulk of the enemy, however, were in full flight through the town, and ere long the English colours waved from the most elevated building of the palace citadel.

Establishing his head-quarters in one of the bastions overlooking the town, and keeping the left attacking-column to hold what had been acquired, the General pushed on the other two columns to obtain possession of the town itself.

They advanced by different streets, and—as the weakness of the firing indicated—with but slight opposition. Dispirited and crestfallen by the capture of their stronghold, the rebel force made no vigorous effort to hold the town. Their aim now was to get clear away, and seek other scenes and pastures new for the exercise of their martial instincts.

> ' He who fights and runs away,
> Lives to fight another day,'

was a principle on which the mutineers acted with praiseworthy consistency.

Deemed to be utterly scattered and broken, the remnants of a beaten and hard-punished force would frequently reassemble with a marvellous rapidity and cohesive power, and reappear in strength in a new district, and, perhaps, again supply themselves with guns and war-material by suddenly pouncing on some loyal Rajah.

Their star was evidently not in the ascendant in the country held by the Hussunabad field-force. They recognized this, and now sought to transfer themselves to other regions where it might become more so. But there were considerable difficulties in their way on this occasion.

'Firing seems almost entirely to have ceased,' observed the General, 'except in the direction of St Clair. I wonder if Colonel Deane has got possession of the

Delhi gate.'

'I'll soon find out, sir,' said Percy, who thought but lightly of his present inactivity, and, in accordance with the constitutional defect to which I have already adverted, desired a little more of the excitement of danger.

The General accepted the offer with an exhortation to be cautious. He had not liked actually to send any one of his staff alone on so dangerous an errand, but was glad to accept it when volunteered.

Percy accordingly mounted, and cantered off through the gate which led into the town. The streets at first seemed to be deserted. What remained of the peaceful inhabitants had retired into their inmost sanctuaries. And, though a few rebel soldiers probably still lingered here and there, the main body had evacuated the place.

Expecting at every turn to be attacked or fired on from some window, Percy pressed on, passing occasionally a dead or wounded man. Some of these were evidently mere peaceful townspeople. But the British soldier-mind at such times regards one dusky face much as another, and fails to discriminate between combatants and non-combatants.

There were two of the dead which struck the thoughtless but compassionate lad who galloped past them, as exhibiting the more repulsive aspect of war.

In one part of the street lay a poor old

gray-headed man, evidently of the trading class. He lay on his back with his face upturned to heaven, and his hands clenching the earth, which he had gripped in his death agony.

Another, also old, was lying half burnt, and with the clothes still on fire. He particularly noticed these as being gentle-looking old men, unmistakably non-combatants.

Soon he passed living townspeople, who, with clasped hands, prayed for mercy and consideration. They asserted that they were only too glad to find the rebel forces driven out. They had been enemies to them, and fleeced by them thoroughly.

Percy was by no means a fluent Hindustanee scholar, indeed his knowledge of the language was of the most limited description, but he endeavoured to pacify the wretched creatures with a few passing words of kindness.   His gentle manner in speaking to them had probably more effect than the ill-understood words themselves.

Gaining from them some information regarding the route of the columns, he still pressed on, and shortly overtook the column of the original right attack, considerably diminished in numbers however.

There marched Mr Seely, still in a sound skin, and conscious of the dignity of being in command of his company—the light one of the regiment he belonged to. Brief words of greeting between the acquaintances served to convey their mutual congratulations.

'Skin watertight?' asked Mr Percy.

'Tight as a drum,' was the reply. 'By the way, you don't happen to have such a thing as "the monkey" about you, have you? This is awfully thirsty work.'

Percy fumbled in one of his holsters, and after a moment or two drew forth 'the monkey,' from where it reposed on a bed of sandwiches.

It had, too, as near neighbours three hard-boiled eggs, some loose bullets, a small powder-flask, a pair of buckskin gloves, and a cheroot case.

'Have a bite also,' he said, handing over some of the above edibles along with 'the monkey.' 'Now I must be off to speak to the Colonel.'

Colonel Deane was leading the column on foot when Percy joined him.

Even as he did so, and delivered his orders, the roar of a gun close on the flank announced the neighbourhood of a battery; and a round shot came crashing into the column from a street they were passing at right angles.

Another and another followed, as a company was wheeled, and dashed up the street towards the town wall from whence the shot had come.

But the gunners did not wait to be attacked. Some by ropes slid down the wall, and made their way as quickly as possible across the open ground beyond,

affording some fine running shooting practice for the Enfield rifles.   Others actually
jumped over, rather than face the British
onslaught, and lay dead or writhing at the
foot of the wall.

The battery was found to consist of two
tolerably heavy brass guns, and a small
shed adjacent containing the ammunition.

Directing a small party to spike or
upset the guns, Colonel Deane pursued
his way to the farther extremity of the
town, but had not proceeded far when an
explosion occurred at the battery he had
just left.

This was immediately followed by the
appearance of several men rushing after
the column, screaming, with clothes on

fire, and faces blackened with gunpowder. The water-carriers, who always accompany a force in India, poured the contents of their skins over the poor wretches, while their comrades tore off the burning clothes. Unable, however, to bear the agony, one or two rushed wildly to the river, and leaping in, disappeared.

Some had met with instant death by the explosion of the magazine, which, whether it were the result of accident or a device of the enemy, none could say.

This, for a short while, delayed the further advance. But it was soon resumed, and the outermost gate reached and occupied. Stands of arms, ready piled, and rice still boiling, gave evident

indications that the rapid progress of the
troops had taken the enemy by surprise,
and hastened their evacuation. In fact,
the town was now in the hands of the
assailants, for the other principal gate had
been captured by the second column. It
now only remained to deal with straggling
bands, who still occupied, and held out in,
a few selected positions within the walls.
Some of these were subsequently battered
down or blown up, and others carried
by assault. In the mean time, however,
it behoved Mr Percy to return to the
General, and report the capture of the
place. More stretchers were required,
too, for the conveyance to hospital of the
wounded. Being the only officer mounted,
he volunteered this latter duty, and gal-

loped back along the streets.

He saw several of the enemy, but they fled at his approach. In one place, however, the townspeople had got hold of one or two of the rebel soldiers, and having disarmed them, were belabouring them with sticks to their hearts' content. In this amusement Percy did not attempt to interfere, but made them give some water to a rebel Sepoy, who lay with shattered leg, and who was in vain imploring drink from a reviling cluster of townsmen gathered about him.

The hazardous ride back was fortunately accomplished without any serious hindrance; and, to the General's deep satisfaction, Percy reported the complete success of the assaulting columns, and the capture of the entire place.

'Well done, Ned!' said Dr Cruickshanks, as they rode after the General into the town. 'Glad to see you back. You must have the bump of combativeness strongly developed. You seemed really to enjoy going off on your errand.

"Thy head is as full of quarrels as an egg is full of meat."

But the devil takes care of his own.'

But Percy, for once, would not rise to chaff. He was thinking of those screaming men on fire.

CHAPTER VIII.

'Imagine something purer far,
    More free from stain of clay
Than Friendship, Love, or Passion are,
    Yet human still as they :
And if thy lip for love like this
    No mortal word can frame,
Go, ask of angels what it is,
    And call it by that name !'
                        Moore's Ballads.

WHILE these events were taking place within the walls of the town, let us see what was going on outside.

St Clair safely received the intimation of the capture of the citadel, and anxiously looked for the evacuation of the entire place by the defeated garrison.

Unfortunately, between the two roads which it was his business especially to watch, lay numerous groves, gardens, and fields, interspersed with many temples and garden-houses. These were eminently adapted to cover the flight of infantry, but the very reverse for the action of cavalry, or the employment of field-guns.

It was not long before indications of the enemy's flight were observed. First came a few straggling horsemen, then larger bodies of mixed horse and foot shortly followed by a few light guns; and then came pell-mell, men, horses, camels, bullocks, carts, all pouring out of the further gate in the greatest disorder, each apparently intent only on outstripping the others. The terrible 'hoorah' of the dreaded soldier people was heard in the distance behind them, and hastened the confused exodus.

The guns were soon taken by a charge of the cavalry, and left standing in the road deserted. The rebel cavalry were next attacked and dispersed—numbers of them flinging themselves off their horses and seeking the shelter of the gardens. Attention was then turned to the infantry, and such as still kept to the more open country were easily disposed of. But the bulk of the fugitives was scattered through the enclosed lands, where they made rapid progress, and generally set the attacking cavalry at defiance.

St Clair, however, with a select body
of the best mounted, managed to keep in
sight a leader, who was evidently a man
of mark, and escorted by a chosen band.
He was one of those who, together with
his adherents, had hastily abandoned their
horses and sought in that way to elude
the pursuers. But St Clair had noted him.
It was of great importance to capture the
principal chiefs, and this might be such,
perhaps the Rajah himself. So, over
hedges, walls, and all other obstructions
he managed with a few followers to pursue
the object of his suspicions, who was
evidently but ill-accustomed to such very
active exercise in his own person. This
was evident from the exertions of those
about him, by whom he was pulled, and

pushed, and hustled through and over all sorts of obstacles, until at last, utterly exhausted, he was seen to hold some brief council with his followers. This shortly resulted in their taking refuge in one of the country houses I have mentioned.

St Clair, with the pursuing party, soon arrived in the vicinity of the spot, and distributing a few of his men so as to keep watch all round, he prepared to take further measures for attacking the house.

Selecting a grove of trees at some distance from the contemplated scene of operations, he led his men to it, and ordered them to dismount and picket their horses. Leaving a few in charge, he divided the rest of the party into two bands. One of these he placed under the command of young Stanford, who had accompanied him, with directions to skirmish towards the back of the house, and keep up a sharp fire on the doors and windows. At the head of the other he placed himself; and after improvising a sort of battering-ram, which consisted simply of a heavy log of wood slung on some spare horse-tether ropes, he conducted his men by a circuitous route, taking advantage of whatever cover offered, until he reached a wall opposite the entrance to the house.

He was now within about one hundred yards of the object of attack, and carefully reconnoitred both it and the ground he would have to clear before reaching it.

The house was a low, one-storied building, with many small windows, from which a continual musketry-fire was kept up. The door was closed, and St Clair judged, from its appearance, would readily give way before a few applications of his battering-ram.

To admit of the passage of this, a breach was very quickly broken in the frail mud wall which sheltered them; and St Clair, at the head of his party, made the best of his way across the intervening space direct towards the door.

On they rushed as fast as the carriage of the log permitted them, losing a few of their number from the fire which was now concentrated upon them. The skirmishers also closed in, endeavouring to keep down the fire from the house at shorter range than hitherto.

St Clair had nearly reached the door when he felt a sharp and sudden shock, and his left arm fell powerless to his side. Quickly recovering from the stinging sensation of the blow and the momentary falter in his progress which it occasioned, he dashed up to the door. In a few seconds the battering-ram was brought into play, and, under the simultaneous impulse of a dozen sturdy pairs of hands, swung backwards and forwards with crashing violence against the somewhat frail obstruction. A few blows sufficed. Panels, lock, and hinges all gave way, and the door was dashed in, leaving free ingress to the assailants—free, at least, as regarded such inanimate obstacle.

But the defenders were evidently determined not to be taken without a vigorous struggle, and resolved to sell their lives as dearly as possible.

After directing those of his men unemployed with the battering-ram, to pour a volley into the now open passage, St Clair rushed in through the thick smoke, closely followed, sword in hand, by eager soldiers.

For some brief moments he met with no opposition ; and the thick smoke so obscured everything a few feet distant that he could not see his enemies. But not long was his course unobstructed.

At the corner of a passage and entrance to a room he came in collision with the defenders, and here the conflict

became a downright hand-to-hand struggle.   Emptied carbines were thrown aside
or used as clubs, but swords formed the
principal weapons both of attack and defence.

The first man they met went down
before St Clair's sword-thrust; but, in
return, his comrade cut at the Englishman before the latter could recover his
weapon, only in his turn to feel the keen,
incisive blow of the Sikh native officer
who was now almost abreast with his
superior.

The hot smart and spurt of blood from
temple and cheek roused the devil, which,
however subdued, is seldom entirely absent
from a nature so vigorous as that of St
Clair.   Onward he pressed, cutting and

hewing his way with a fierceness which, from its unusual display, was the more to be dreaded. His commanding stature and great muscular power, added to unusual skill as a swordsman, bore down all opposition, or induced his opponents to avoid his terrible onslaught, and seek among his followers other foemen worthy of their steel, though less terrible to encounter.

Midst the din and tumult of the strife, its clash of arms, and shouts, groans, and imprecations, St Clair heard occasional words of command issue from one whose appearance he could only indistinctly see in the smoke and dust of the fray. Towards him, however, he fought his way from one room to another, as, pressed back by superior numbers and strength, the rebel band retreated.

At last St Clair's perseverance was rewarded, and he found himself face to face with the leader, who he now saw was none other than the Rajah.

'Surrender,' shouted St Clair to him. 'Further fighting is useless. You cannot escape.'

'I can die as becomes a Rajpoot chief,' was the reply, as he rushed forward and aimed a cut at his adversary.

This was parried, and, with one vigorous blow in return, St Clair cut down on the turbaned head of his assailant. So violent was the blow that, though the cleft turban somewhat protected the skull, the wearer was felled to the ground, and his conqueror stood over him.

With the fall of their chief his adherents gave up further resistance, though
several of them were cut down in the
heat and excitement of the encounter
even after opposition had ceased. St
Clair's stentorian order to 'spare, not
slay,' soon, however, put an end to indis-
criminate slaughter.

During the few brief minutes which
had elapsed from the time of entrance
into the house to the overthrow of the
chief, St Clair had been upheld by the
excitement and stimulus of action. But
now that the immediate object of self-
sustainment no longer existed, and there
remained no influence to distract his attention from himself, he felt that his

wounds were serious.

The prisoners, including the chief, were secured, and St Clair was at leisure to turn his attention to his own wounds and those of his companions.

His faithful soldiers were soon eagerly inquiring into the nature of the 'great Major Sahib's' hurts, for the upper part of his person was covered with the blood which flowed from his gashed face. A deep cut across brow and cheek, fortunately avoiding the eye, proved the most distressing to look at, but much the less serious of his two wounds, for it was found that the bone of the left arm was shattered above the elbow.

The house itself, which was a summer 'palace of delight,' belonging to the chief,

was turned into a temporary hospital.
There, amid the pleasant groves and
gardens, and in the rooms with their
elaborately-decorated walls, carved wood-
work, and luxurious garnishing, now lay
men dead and wounded.

Full often had it echoed to the voices
of the nautch girls, the notes of the native
guitar, and other instruments of music,
and all the varied sounds of native li-
centiousness and revelry. The nature of
its uses and belongings, and the soft and
enervating atmosphere which pervaded
the place, were strangely at variance with
the turmoil of strife and the tempest of
men's angry passions which had but
lately resounded through it. But this
transformation it had undergone. Its

polished mortar floors were obscured with blood, rendering them, contrary to literary formula, less slippery than heretofore.

And not less strange in contrast to its original character was its subsequent adoption as a general hospital, where the groans of pain and contortions of agony replaced the amatory songs and graceful but lascivious motions of the nautch girls.

It was evening before Percy heard of his friend's wounds.

Having returned with the General to the citadel, he was at that precise time engaged with others in exploring the underground regions of the palace, where he fully expected to find those stacks of jewels, and other valuables, of which he had heard.

But the search was not so satisfactory as he had hoped. Indeed, he came to the conclusion that the proceeds by no means compensated for the stuffiness and confined nature of the region in which the investigation was conducted. This he compared—in his own peculiar phraseology—in point of restricted accommodation and absence of fresh air, to 'the marine apartments occupied by Mr Jonah during his short sojourn in the depths of the sea.'

Immediately on receiving intelligence of the state of St Clair, he hurried off and obtained leave from the General to visit and remain with the 'dear old man' during the night. But that night was prolonged into many subsequent ones.

The surgeons were obliged to remove the wounded arm, and during the fever which ensued, Percy proved a gentle and attentive, if no very skilful, attendant. And, perhaps, the most difficult and arduous of his duties was the writing of the daily bulletin which was sent to 'Nora Creina,' as he continued to call his friend's *fiancée*.

But the force was long detained at Sungumpore; and at length Percy had the satisfaction of announcing that St Clair was out of danger, and progressing towards convalescence. But, alas! he had only escaped from the valley of the shadow of death with the loss of an arm, and a gash across his face which sadly marred what had not before been beautiful to look on.

In his juvenile inexperience of the tender loyalty of a true woman who really loves, and exaggerating the advantages of personal appearance, which will, at his age, have great sway, Percy held doubting communion with himself regarding the effect his friend's disfigurement might possibly have on Norah. Indeed, so unsatisfactory were his cogitations on this subject, when he reflected on these drawbacks, added to the 'awful age of the old man'—the latter was just eight and thirty—that he determined to consult his friend, Dr Cruickshanks, for whose opinion on such matters he really entertained some respect.

He 'didn't doubt the girl, but somehow he—' In fact, he could not express his ideas in any very lucid or satisfactory manner.

The worthy doctor, however, had little difficulty in reading the nature of what were rather doubts than fears in his young friend's breast; and, as usual, brought a text from Shakspeare to bear on the question.

After listening quietly to the young fellow's description of his sentiments, he said, 'All right, Ned, I understand. Don't you alarm yourself. She is one of those who is loving and constant as she is pure and good. As for difference in age, so much the better. I have got a very fitting quotation to meet the case. Here you are, my boy :—

" Let still the woman take
An elder than herself ; so wears she to him,
So sways she level in her husband's heart :
For, boy, however we do praise ourselves,
Our fancies are more giddy and infirm,
More longing, wavering, sooner lost and worn,
Than women's are." '

Greatly priding himself on the unusual aptness of his quotation, the doctor
chuckled, and affirmed that, whatever the
nature of the subject, ' glorious Will was
equal to the occasion, and had something
to say apposite and conclusive.'

Forgetting even to chaff the doctor,
and considerably reassured by the decided
view thus taken of the case, Percy felt
much relieved in mind, and wrote a long
letter to Nora Creina, describing the
nature of St Clair's wounds, and thus
preparing her for the first sight of his

scarred and altered face. St Clair had been ordered by the surgeons to the sea-coast, and being now able to travel, he was about to depart for Hussunabad *en route.*

And had the principal himself any misgivings? He had little that any real or permanent change in her love would be wrought by his altered appearance. But he could not divest himself of a growing disquietude regarding the effect of the shock on a nature so sensitive as hers. He pictured to himself, with a terrible species of fascination, the start of horror and of momentary aversion which would cross her face when she first saw him. Perhaps, indeed, subsequently also.

It was in this frame of mind and that mixture of happy anticipation and anxious dread which a man of sensitive feeling and diffident nature, in his circumstances, might be supposed to feel, that he rode slowly in to Hussunabad one morning.

He was surprised and disappointed at finding that no one rode out to meet him. But his village messenger, despatched from the previous night's halting ground, had either lost the letter intrusted to him, or deeming his own convenience of more importance than its delivery, had never ventured beyond the confines of his village, but returned to the bosom of his family.

During the absence of the force, the

Residency had been repaired and re-
occupied; and thither St Clair bent his
way, according to previous invitation.

'Yes, both the burra sahib and the
missee sahib had come in from their
morning ride,' said the servant he addressed. 'The mem sahib was in the
morning-room alone at present, preparing
the tea.'

Thither he was conducted, and, for
one brief moment, stood trembling and
irresolute on the threshold of the room,
as the servant retired after announcing
him. He felt the seam on his face throb.
Then he stepped forward and received
within the fold of his solitary arm, a
slight figure which rushed towards him
and threw its arms round his neck, crying

out as it did so, 'Darling, darling, you are given back to me.'

Did he see that look of horror or aversion his imagination had pictured ? Did she appear shocked during the brief space in which he was able to scan her features before they were too close to be noted minutely ?

He perceived nothing of either. But what he did perceive was the tenderest look of pity which, he thought, he had ever seen on a human face. And yet the poor child had for days been schooling herself to suppress all outward signs of her deep compassion. She feared it might, in some inexplicable way, hurt his masculine sensitiveness ; and yet she wished him to feel that his loss the more endeared him to her. As to any expression of distaste or repugnance at this sight of his maimed and scarred figure, it had not entered into her imagination; or if, in her natural womanly dislike to look on such, the thought had occurred to her, it was only to be at once and for ever suppressed. She would rather have given a limb of her own than shown any feeling of that nature to him.

'Then, my own loved child,' he said after the first embrace, as he laid his hand on her head and made her look up at him,—'then you are not frightened or shocked at this,' and he held up his empty sleeve, ' or this hideous scar ! '

She looked full at both, steadfastly, loyally, without any indication of shrinking, and her first answer was to pull down the head and press her lips upon the disfiguring scar which seamed his face. And then she spoke : ' Frightened ! shocked ! no, my own dearest. What should shock me in that way ? I only feel such great pity for your loss. I may do that, may I not ? '

' Yes,' he said. ' But is it mingled with no feeling of aversion towards this maimed and hideous wreck ? '

' I will not have you speak in that way. It is not a maimed and hideous wreck. It contains what I love above everything in the world. What signifies to me a change in its outward semblance ? It contains the same spirit as before, and which has touched mine. That is what I love.'

'But think. There is this frightful scar, this terrible mutilation.'

'I would rather have you as you are than if you were in full strength. If it were not in pity for what you must feel for your loss, I could rejoice; because you are so much more to me.'

'So much more to you! How?' he inquired.

'I can be of so much more use, I can help you now. Your own little child can be your poor left arm, and supply the want its loss has created. Don't you see, Hugh, my own darling, that I can be so much more now, can serve you and be more of your second self?'

'This is woman's love, is it?' he said, in a soft, subdued voice.

'Yes,' she replied simply. 'Men, even men like you, don't quite understand it, I fancy, till sorrow or distress comes. Why, if you had been utterly prostrated by your wounds, don't you think I should have continued to love you just the same? No, more! I could have been a nurse and comforter, and felt that I could be so much more to you than I can be to a strong, active man.'

'This is woman's love!' he repeated, as he looked fondly down at her earnest, pleading face. 'It seems to me that the word angelic might not be altogether mis-placed.'

'You mustn't say that,' she quickly rejoined. 'It *would* be misplaced. It is perhaps more of our womanly selfishness to have all one loves to oneself, and be everything and all to the loved one.'

' Such utter self-abnegation and craving to be of help is a sort of selfishness which the world would much benefit by if more commonly exercised,' he said. ' I have ever thought highly of a good, pure-minded woman's love. But I was not quite prepared for one such as you describe, my own dearly-loved little one. God bless you for it, my own cherished darling.'

It was in this way that the indications of the aversion he dreaded to discover exhibited itself.

CONCLUSION.

' And the stately ships go on
  To their haven under the hill ;
But oh for the touch of a vanish'd hand,
  And the sound of a voice that is still ! '
                                    TENNYSON.

I HAVE little to add to my simple
narrative.

St Clair was advised to seek the invigorating climate of old England to
recruit his strength, and he readily obtained leave on medical certificate.

The Selbys and Mrs Atherton accompanied him home. The wear and tear of

those anxious months had wrought their influence on Mr Selby ; and now that the storm was weathered, he considered that he had earned a right to take his rest.

So the little party journeyed on their way, held together in the bonds of a common friendship, though with the light and shade of joy and sorrow somewhat unequally distributed.

Norah was quietly happy in the society of the man she so deeply loved. And her little efforts at ministering to him, and really replacing the loss he had sustained, were received with the profoundest sense of admiring interest and gratitude. And he would sometimes invent wants on purpose to see the pleasure it gave her to meet them.

But while thus attentive to him who was shortly to become her husband, she never lost sight of the sorrow of her friend. She never ceased, with feminine tact and delicacy, to help and comfort her in that undemonstrative way which true sympathy learns in attempting to solace an irremediable grief.

Not unmixed, therefore, was her happiness, or indeed that of any member of the party, for all had to mourn the loss of friends.

Full freighted with sorrow and human agony of every description were the mail steamers and homeward-bound ships in those days. Never, probably, did a campaign close with so much of cause for misery. For, in addition to the long public rolls of killed and wounded in battle, inseparable from war, there existed those of the first victims of the great mutiny of both sexes and all ages. And, alas! even to these must still further be added the unpublished lists of nameless sorrows.

England was safely reached, and in due time Norah Selby became Mrs St Clair.

But before taking leave of my readers I must once more refer to one in whom I hope they have taken some little interest —Ned Percy.

To use an expression common at the time, 'the neck of the mutiny was broken,' but there was yet much to be done in eradicating the various shoots which, like the offspring of that Indian tree, took root apart from the parent trunk.

By the middle of 1858 all serious opposition and hard fighting was over. But the equally serious and far more trying duty of hunting the fugitive bands yet remained, to exercise those qualities of officers and men which are far rarer than the mere exhibition of courage in action.

Percy was engaged in the pursuit of that *ignis fatuus*, the cowardly, but ubiquitous and celebrated Tantia Topee. And he had some very fair opportunities of judging what real hard work was. His experiences in that respect were gained both during the hot weather, with the thermometer occasionally in tents at 120°, and in the cold, with it below

freezing point. For 1859 was well advanced before the man we could not
catch was delivered into our hands by
treachery.

It is not, however, with his further
campaigning that I have here to deal,
only with a letter which he received. It
was in reply to one he had written to the
sister of his dear friend, Douglas.

The good-natured lad's eyes were
quite moist as he read it, and from its
contents, realized how strong was the
affection which had subsisted between
brother and sister. But while comment-
ing on the bitterness of her loss, the
writer, at the same time, expressed her
deep sense of gratitude to those who had
been her loved brother's friends, his

chosen companions in his days of health, and mourners for his death.

It was couched in terms of deep and vigorous feeling, and, withal, so unaffected that it made a strong impression on the reader.

'What an awfully jolly letter!' he murmured as he laid it down on his camp-table, and silently regarded it. 'And what a dear, jolly little thing she must be—and only just sixteen too!' he reflected, after a pause, as he called to mind a likeness of her with age and date affixed which he had seen in Douglas' possession.

Again he read the letter over, and then carefully folding it, locked it up in the battered case which did duty for his desk. It was an honour he accorded to very few letters indeed; for in his estimation they were ordinarily only written to be read and destroyed.

It only remains for me to speak of Mrs Atherton. Time with its healing influence came to her as to others to assuage the poignancy of her sorrow for Douglas' loss. Handsome, well-endowed, and still young, she found, after awhile, no lack of those who would willingly have attempted to cultivate more intimate relations, and persuade her to forget the dead in interest for the living. But she encouraged none. The deepest affections of her heart lay buried in the distant grave under the lime-tree in the Hussunabad church-yard, where he lay at rest.

Her best love could never, ah! never be withdrawn from the gallant soldier whose noblest victory had been gained for her sake—the triumph over himself; whose real 'cross of honour' was unstained by ambition or any vulgar craving for public applause.

Remorse for that one false step was in time replaced by the chastened regret which accompanied that sin's deep repentance. But the regret was passionate and deathless.

Her love had passed away, lamenting that one deviation from the strict path of virtuous principle and purity of conduct into which her weakness in the hour of passion had led her. That could never be forgotten or put aside, because it had lightened her in his estimation, and defaced the idol of purity he had set up.

She greatly altered. She became very gentle, and her proud nature far humbler; and in time she came to recognize that her spirit had issued, purified and cleansed of much dross, from the ordeal she had undergone. She understood that the burden imposed on her was that whose chastening influence her rebellious nature most required.

Years after, in speaking of these sad days, she acknowledged that, even in this world, to the weary in spirit there may come rest and peace, and that modified happiness which trials prepare the tried more fully to appreciate. But it was long before she was able fully to perceive that

' Our angels oft greet us in tearful guise,
  And our saviours come in sorrow ;
  While the murkiest midnight that frowns from the skies
  Is at heart a radiant morrow.'

With her disreputable father she held as little personal intercourse as possible, and he was contented to receive the sum she annually allowed him in lieu of it.

To Lilly Douglas she became sincerely attached, and gained the entire love and trust of the young girl. It gave her a new interest in life ; and she watched, with an almost maternal solicitude, the development of her character. Much she told her of the last days of him whose memory was so dear to both. She showed her ring and its inscription, and she frequently spoke of the faithful manner in which he had acted up to the spirit of his

pledge.   But she could never bring herself to narrate the actual circumstances
which had so severely tried that honour
of which it was the gage.

THE END.

JOHN CHILDS AND SON, PRINTERS.

www.ingramcontent.com/pod-product-compliance
Lightning Source LLC
Chambersburg PA
CBHW031334070726
47496CB00018B/1856